SEVENTEEN STORIES

Seventeen Stories

by

Mark Valentine

Swan River Press
Dublin, Ireland
MMXXI

Seventeen Stories
by Mark Valentine

Published by
Swan River Press
Dublin, Ireland
in April, MMXXI

www.swanriverpress.ie
brian@swanriverpress.ie

Cover design by Meggan Kehrli from
"A Door in Florence" (2013) by Jason Zerrillo

Set in Garamond by Ken Mackenzie

Paperback Edition
ISBN 978-1-78380-743-7

Swan River Press published a limited hardback
edition of *Seventeen Stories* in October 2013.

Contents

Four Haunted Figures

In Memoriam
Roger Dobson
Ave Atque Vale

Three Singular Detectives

The Adventure of the Green Skull

I have mentioned before the three massive manuscript volumes that contain my notes on our cases for the year 1894. Circumstances now allow me to reveal the details of one of these, as weird and tragic a case as any we encountered. It was, I see, the beginning of November, and Holmes was on capital form, pleased to be back at the hub of matters in London after his long incognito wanderings in the East and elsewhere. There had been a high wind wailing outside our rooms and throughout the city, and Holmes was just beginning to become restless for some new matter to whet his keen mind upon. As was his habit, therefore, he was scouring the pages of *The Times* at breakfast, seeking evidence of anything untoward. Today his researches had an especial edge, for he had received word that Inspector Lestrade would call later, if convenient.

"Read that, Watson," he said, passing the paper to me, and pointing to a brief paragraph.

" 'Mr. Josiah Walvis, fifty-one, an overseer at the Bow-side match-works, met an untimely end on Saturday evening when he fell from a high wall abutting the East India Wharf, and cracked his skull. The cause of his sad accident has not been ascertained. It is understood Mr. Walvis had been entertaining friends at the Lamb & Flag public house before making his way home. Interviewed, his associates say the deceased was of his normal disposition upon departing, and was not excessively inebriated. It is considered possible Mr. Walvis

11

was contemplating a shorter route to his home but missed his footing. Two witnesses, a watchman and a street boy, aver that they saw the victim pursued some moments beforehand, but this cannot be better corroborated. The proprietor of the Bow match-works reports that Mr. Walvis was a diligent and just employee who—well, etc., etc.' "

"There is the barest hint of promise in that, Watson: the pursuer, you know. But it is otherwise a drab affair. Yet it is all there is. Inventive evil appears to have quite vanished from London."

Holmes sighed, and began to gather up the dottles for his morning pipe.

ℰꝋ

The visit of our colleague from Scotland Yard did not at first obviate his gloom. For it seemed Lestrade had indeed nothing better to offer.

"It's the Walvis business, Mr. Holmes."

"Oh, indeed? But that happened two days ago, Lestrade. The gales will have rushed all the evidence to the four corners. There is no point in coming to me now."

"Well, it seems a straightforward case that is hardly worth your while. But one of the constables, a keen lad, saw something he didn't quite like."

"Indeed?"

"Yes. Of course, an accident is quite the likeliest explanation. There was no robbery, and no other marks on the body but those caused by the fall. Yet, here is the thing: in the deceased's left hand, between the two middle fingers, protruding outwards, was a spent match."

"Ah. That is singular." I saw my friend's eyes gleam.

"Quite so. A drowning man may clutch at a straw, but—I say to myself—a falling man does not. He splays his fingers, so . . . "

"Therefore, the match was placed there after the fall," I interjected.

"Exactly, Doctor," returned Lestrade. "Now I am inclined to regard it as merely a macabre little joke on the part of the friends who found him. They all worked at the match factory, you know. They were pretty far gone in drink. So they put it there as if to say 'you, Walvis, have struck your last match'. I questioned them pretty fiercely about that, but they deny it. Half didn't notice it at all, the others say it must have blown there . . . "

"You have preserved the match, Lestrade?" Holmes demanded.

"I have, Mr. Holmes, and—knowing your ways—have brought it with me." Lestrade produced a twist of paper from his waistcoat pocket and handed it over.

Holmes inspected the exhibit carefully between thumb and forefinger, then handed it back.

"It tells us little. It is a Lyphant & Bray match—the people who have the Bow works. So it could well have come from his colleagues. Or from almost anybody. It is a very popular brand. Yet, someone who has handled it may be an actor."

We both looked suitably astonished, and Holmes favoured us with an explanation. "It is very simple. I have studied the shape, size and composition of over forty types of lucifer or match—the matter complements my researches upon tobacco ash, you know. A combination of a certain ash and a certain match may help to mark a man. But not in this case. No ash, and a very common brand."

"The theatrical connection?" I urged.

Holmes shrugged. "Oh, merely that someone has left a small smudge of greasepaint upon the stick. Not you or your constable, I assume, Lestrade?"

"Indeed not."

"Well, it does not get us very far. But what about this evidence of a pursuer, Inspector?"

Our visitor's face settled into a satisfied smirk.

"The witnesses are not very sound. An aged watchman, half deaf and almost wholly foolish. A street arab, with a lively imagination."

"And what do they say?"

"Well, Mr. Holmes, I don't give it much credit. Indeed, I am trying what I can to suppress their little yarn. It doesn't take much to spread unreasoning terror abroad."

There was a brittle silence, Lestrade savouring the matter that had really brought him to us, Holmes quiveringly alert.

"They say they saw Walvis chased down the street by a phantom. It wore a hooded cloak, but they caught a glimpse of its face—if you can call it that. It looked more like, they said, it looked more like—a green skull."

Sherlock Holmes rose from his chair and rubbed his hands together. "Come now," he said. "This sounds promising."

℞

The case may have caught my friend's imagination, because of its peculiarities, but for some days he made little progress. The scene, as he had anticipated, had been quite wiped clean by the wind and rain of the intervening days, and all the witnesses he interviewed stuck resolutely to the stories they had given the police, even the two who had seen the spectral pursuer. Lyphant & Bray would give nothing but a sound character to Walvis, conceding only that by some he might be regarded as somewhat stern in his duties. There was little more for Holmes to do, and he was succumbing again to his blue devils when, barely a week later, Mrs. Hudson ushered in a new client. He was an angular, brisk young man, pale and peremptory in manner.

℞

"Sit down, Mr. Reynolds. This is my friend and associate, Dr. Watson. What is your business with us?"

"I have read of you, Mr. Holmes, from Dr. Watson's accounts. I have observed that you see importance in matters others overlook."

"You are very kind. And you think you have a similar matter?"

"I do. My employer, Mr. Thomas Mostyn died last night."

"I see. The cause?"

"Heart failure."

Holmes looked crestfallen.

"It is certain?"

"Yes. His medical man has treated him for years. He has long had indifferent health. I could see this for myself too."

"Then why—?"

"That was the *cause* of his death, Mr. Holmes. I am concerned about the *occasion* of it."

"There is something here that does not satisfy you?"

"A number of matters."

Holmes tapped his fingers upon the arm of his chair.

"Pray proceed."

"Mr. Mostyn's face in death was distorted most disturbingly. It was a grimacing mask, exhibiting naked fear."

I interrupted. "Rictus, Mr. Reynolds. It can give the most distressing effects."

Our client turned to me. "I understand. But there is rather more. Though in his nightgown and dressing-gown, as if prepared for bed, Mr. Mostyn met his end in his study. Some matter had taken him there. And in death he was clutching between his middle fingers, pointing outwards—"

"A match."

Mr. Reynolds's face was a picture of astonishment. "Great heavens, yes! How did you know?"

Holmes smiled. "No matter. It was used?"

"Yes."

"Well, perhaps he was about to enjoy a cigar before retiring. It is not uncommon."

"Certainly not, Mr. Holmes. My employer disapproved of smoking. It was the only matter of disagreement between us. If I wished to smoke, I must do so clandestinely."

"I see. He does not sound very companionable. Well, Mr. Reynolds, let us have more of your story. You are his private secretary?"

"I am. I deal—I dealt—with nearly all his business and personal correspondence. He has many financial interests. I have been with him some seven years, since I successfully answered an advertisement he had placed upon his return from Guiana. He was reticent about his wealth, but that he had made a very great deal in the Americas was evident enough to me from his investments."

"And had made enemies, no doubt?"

"I never heard of any. Indeed, all of his affairs appeared to me almost entirely untroubled, until—well, that is, until the particular incident that brings me to you. On Tuesday last week, I opened Mr. Mostyn's correspondence as usual, and there was nothing out of the ordinary run of things, but one: an envelope that contained no letter, only a handful of matches. I could not imagine what the sender's purpose was, although sometimes the advertisement men do try the most foolish tricks to engage attention. I threw it in the basket. When I took in the rest of the day's post and went through it with my employer, we dealt with it all well enough, until—at the end—I mentioned the matches, light-heartedly. Quite a remarkable change came over his face. I had never seen him so agitated, except perhaps once when he felt he had been browbeaten by a hothead of a lawyer into some settlement he did not like—the one matter, as it happens, where he did not confide in me."

"I see. The envelope arrived—what, eight days ago? Go on, Mr. Reynolds. This may all be more germane than you know."

"In his agitation, Mr. Mostyn asked me exactly how many matches there were. I am afraid I laughed and said I did not know. He became vehement and told me to go and count them at once. I could scarcely believe the order, but I did as he bid."

"And?"

"There were nine or ten."

"Nine *or* ten? Mr. Reynolds!"

"Ten, then. It seemed of no moment."

"Do you have them?"

"Well, yes I do. But only because I found them in my employer's desk drawer, next to his appointments diary. I cannot imagine why he kept them."

Our visitor handed them over and Holmes subjected them to scrutiny, separating three from the others.

Mr. Reynolds regarded Holmes's actions quizzically, then resumed. "A little later that day, Mr. Mostyn gave me a most unusual instruction. He said that business compelled him to go abroad again, it might be for some time. I was to realise as much as I could, and as quickly as I could, of his investments, so that within one week—he was most insistent upon that—within one week, he should be ready to leave."

"He had never done such a thing before?"

"No. I was very much surprised. From what I knew of his business affairs, there was nothing of any consequence to call his attention overseas. But by requiring me to turn his holdings to cash so quickly, he forfeited a great deal of their value. I could not imagine what would impel him to that."

"Is there anything more, Mr. Reynolds?"

Our visitor hesitated.

"No."

"Think back very carefully, sir. Over this recent period, has there been any matter whatever at all out of the ordinary?"

"Oh, only foolish talk from the boot-boy. He reads too much sensational literature."

"Indeed? I find it has much to commend it. And what was his prattle? Spring-Heeled Jack? The Wild Boys of the Sewers?"

"Ha, very nearly so, Mr. Holmes. He said he saw some figure skulking around the garden at night. He has an attic room that commands a view. He should have been asleep, but no doubt was reading his rubbish. He said he saw Death with a lantern. The maid, superstitious soul, says it had come for Mr. Mostyn. I had to speak severely to both of them . . . Of course, there may have been an interloper, but scarcely in that form. Now, Mr. Holmes, what is your advice?"

"I should like to visit the scene without delay, Mr. Reynolds. And I am concerned for you, sir. You have had an unpleasant experience. Now there is no necessity for subterfuge, help yourself to one of these—a Macedonian—you will find it quite soothing—while we get ready. Now, where are my matches? You some with you? Good, good. We shall not be long."

ॐ

Despite the tragedy that had taken place in Number 4, Pavia Court, Mostyn's address, I relished our visit, for it was a pleasure to see Holmes prowling throughout the house and its modest grounds in his customary keen-eyed search for any clue that might bring substance to the shadows that had gathered here. I saw him crawling carefully around the garden at the rear, and its narrow entrance gate, examining the sash upon the study window that overlooked it on the ground floor, and walking up and down the small, blind street, itself off a very minor thoroughfare, that comprised the Court, in all these places picking up and examining any piece of unregarded flotsam. I heard of him also in the pantry in animated conversation with Victor, the boot-boy, comparing the merits of various thrilling pamphlets: and in the study, questioning Reynolds closely about his employer's business holdings.

For my part, I sought out Mostyn's doctor, Hawkins, on the pretext that I was a medical advisor to his insurance people. Although, as a matter of form, the district police had been called, they had relied upon his assurance that a heart failure was responsible for the death. He conceded he had quite expected—and indeed hoped, since Mostyn paid well—that his patient would have survived some years longer, but it was still quite within the bounds of medical science that the condition had taken him earlier. Might—I suggested—some additional anxiety in his affairs, even some shock or other, have contributed? Dr. Hawkins was affable: yes, of course, it very well might.

℘

It was clear to me that Holmes had some definite line of enquiry in his sights, though I could not tell what. The next day, he was missing from our rooms for much of the time, and would say only that he had paid a call upon one of the new independent lucifer-makers. I was, therefore, a little taken aback when, shortly after our visit to Mostyn's home, the boot-boy Victor presented himself, somewhat wind-ruffled but evidently bursting with news.

℘

"I did 'sactly as you said, Mr. Holmes. I took a place in the bun shop opposite this inventor cove's place, Raffles, and watched and watched. I had to eat getting on for a dozen stickies before your mark came out, corst a terrible lot they

19

did—" (a clink) "well, thank you very much, sir, anyways after you'd been to see him and he'd shut up shop that day, it was hours and hours after, he looks about him and sets off smartish. But I'm on his track like you told me . . . "

"You see, Watson, nobody ever pays attention to small boys loitering or getting up to mischief. It's what they do. A perfect disguise: behaving naturally. Well, where did (ahem) the inventor Raffles go?"

"He went out Chelsea way, where all the artists and anarchists are, sir. They're always up to plots in *The Black Paper*, 'sfact."

"So they are, Victor. And who are they are in league with eh?"

"That's what I was going to find out. He heads for a door in a yard off Blyth Street, and he's looking all around him, see: furtive, that's what they call it. But he doesn't see me. And he knocks and there's a wait and like a Judas in the door opens, but I can't see much. And then—then the door opens just a crack, and he talks very excited like, and he gets let in. And he stays there not long, twenty minutes maybe."

"See anything when the door opened?"

"You bet. Woundy—beg pardon, sir—scary."

"You're sure, Victor?"

"Blood honour, sir."

"That's good enough for me."

I looked from one to the other. "Well?"

Holmes raised an eyebrow.

"He saw Death, Watson. Isn't that right? The thing that came to Mr. Mostyn's garden?"

The youth nodded solemnly.

ℰℭ

Holmes wasted no time. After swift directions from the boy, amply rewarded, we hailed a cab to the hidden, curious quarter he had indicated. In the neighbourhood, my friend enlisted another ragamuffin helper, a blind match-seller. A sovereign and a swift rehearsal of her role ensued. God knows she was battered enough looking, but she made her condition look even more distressing and knocked weakly and repeatedly at the door, imploring help. At the first the face behind the shutter ushered her away, but she swayed and cried and pleaded. The figure within went away a while, and then the door opened very slowly. We then abandoned all subtlety and flung ourselves at the crack. The child ran off, there was a harsh shout and a scurrying, and we burst in.

We were confronted by—a thing at bay. In one corner of the bare, meanly-furnished room, there stood glowering at us a figure wrapped around in cloaks from which emerged a hairless, shrunken, bony head, where such meagre flesh as there was had a vile, livid hue.

"I do not know who or what you are," Sherlock Holmes said, "but your business is at an end. I have evidence that will connect you with two deaths."

The creature's eyes were filled with hatred, and cast wildly about for escape. Then they seemed to dim, and the skull sank down, before it looked up at us again.

"You have no evidence that would convince a court. Yet perhaps it is time to let things rest. And I believe you will not speak so harshly when you have heard my story."

I gasped, and I could sense that even the icy Holmes was taken aback. For the voice was that of a gentlewoman, clear and well-modulated. She beckoned us to two rough chairs. We made introductions and looked at her enquiringly.

ॐ

"My name is of no consequence. I was born in the colony of Guiana, where my mother succumbed young to the foul waters. My father and a native nursemaid looked after me in my infancy but he was taken too by some disease of the unhealthy conditions there. We had no close kin, but there was a distant cousin who had been once in the colony and had come to know my father before returning to England. I found that I—and my father's wealth—were entrusted to this person, and I was shipped to a land I had never known as home. The next part of my story will hardly surprise you. This cousin and guardian, so called, claimed my father's business affairs were in disorder and it was all he could do to settle his debts, penurying himself in the process. I must be put to work. I was sent to the Lyphant & Bray match factory, and housed nearby in squalid lodgings. From then onwards—I was twelve, mark you—my life was one of unremitting drudgery and callousness, in the most terrible conditions. I saw my guardian infrequently and then, I am sure, he came only to ensure I was secure. The fact that I had been educated and prepared for a gentler place made matters worse. The taskmaster—Walvis—took a hatred of me. I believe he was in league with my guardian, for I saw them confer together when he came. My natural rebelliousness against the conditions meant this creature was able to taunt, scold, fine and beat me. There was not the slightest opportunity I might escape—I was kept under close watch and had no money anyway."

"It is pitiable, Madam," I conceded.

"It is the life of many of your fellow creatures. It would be mine still, had I not taken the one opportunity that came my way. You will recall of course the great match-girls' protest some five or six years ago? I am proud to confess I was one of the agitators. After much hardship, the proprietors permitted a tour of inspection of the factory by some eminent sympathisers—it was all well-managed, of course. But some of the more astute of them realised this, and deliberately looked for an opportunity to become detached from the party and learn the untutored truth. I told my story hurriedly to Mr. Shardlow, the Radical, and he was much affected and promised to see me have justice. I know now that he confronted my guardian and wrung from him some settlement on my behalf—Mr. Shardlow is a lawyer and a strong orator, of course. Since this release, I have done what I can for those left behind. The terrible yellow phosphorous that Lyphant & Bray use must be abolished: there are safer alternatives. That was my campaign. But it will be too late for me."

"You have phossy-jaw, Madam? It is a bad business."

"Exactly, Dr. Watson. You may see the symptoms."

I turned to Holmes. "It affects those over-exposed to the noxious chemicals used in the match trade. It brings a green pallor, a sinking of the cheek bones, complete loss of hair, a shrinking of the flesh. It is incurable. But forgive me, Madam—yours is an exceptionally severe case."

"It is well advanced, Doctor. But also, since I cannot disguise its ravages, I decided to accentuate them, to render my appearance still more ghastly. For I had determined to confront my persecutors face to face with what they had done. With the cunning of theatrical make-up, I thought I could strike terror in their hearts and jolt them into some realisation of their evil. My craft was good. It worked somewhat better than I expected. Poor Walvis fled from me in mad panic and plunged to his doom. While—"

She hesitated.

"Mostyn," supplied Holmes.

"Yes, I see you know everything. Mostyn was already full of fear from the little message I sent him."

"The spent matches," I put in.

"Yes, Doctor. You were my accomplice in those, of course."

"I—why, . . ."

"I read with great relish your account of the 'Five Orange Pips' sent as a sinister warning. And so has half London, I should think. It gave me an idea."

"So I see," remarked Holmes, drily.

"Mostyn was an implacable opponent of the match reforms, and as a chief investor in Lyphant & Bray, was an obstacle to my plans. I had to chase him away. My guardian, I reasoned, would have heard of the strange death of his accomplice, the overseer Walvis. He will not be quite sure if it were the accident it seemed. He will hardly miss the significance of a packet of dead matches delivered to him. And a man less vilely cunning than he would reason that seven matches equals seven days. It was a fair warning. His face when I slid open the sash of his study and advanced upon him was dreadful to behold: yet not, you can see, so dreadful as what he had done to me."

There was a silence.

"And now, gentlemen, what do you intend? You hardly have any case, you know. And it is all one to me. I cannot live much longer: but I would not harm my cause."

Sherlock Holmes stared piercingly at her.

"There must be no more apparitions."

"There will be none."

"Then this matter is concluded. I am my own law, and you are not, as I judge, in default of it."

&

That the case had shaken Holmes I could tell from the brooding silence he observed on our way back to Baker Street in a cab. But once in our rooms again, and after he had played over Swettenham's sweetly melancholy violin sonata, he became somewhat restored.

"I shall be able to use this case in due course as an exemplar for my monograph on lucifers, matches, and spills," he observed. "Here are the ones left on the dead men and sent in the envelope—all Lyphant & Bray—see the squared-off stalks and yellow residue at the head. Here are three that Reynolds cast in the waste basket after having several secret cigarettes—they are identical to the one he left here after smoking one of my Macedonians. They are from the Phoebus Match Co., a rounded stem and a more friable head. They led Mostyn to think he had ten days before Nemesis would strike: in fact, he had only a week.

"And here are those I found in Pavia Court. One at the top of the street, by the sign: struck to check it was the right street; one by the gate; one in the garden, for the dark lantern. These were my treasures. They are a very uncommon match indeed—Raphael's Hygienic. An experimental type, to see if some less deadly form of phosphor can be used in match manufacture, one that will do no harm to the poor creatures in the match manufactories. The lady of the skull, Watson, used Lyphant & Bray, the instruments of her oppression as a calling card on those she wished to harm, but in her everyday use she naturally patronised, and indeed part-funded, the safer design. I merely had to make known that I had connected the apparition to the Raphael workshop, and I felt sure the young inventor there would hurry to let her know and warn her off. In the morning, Watson, I shall visit to reassure him: and, after all we have heard, to place our order for matches always with him."

Prince Zaleski's Secret

I gave my word that this account of the subtle conspiracy against our country in the year 1907 would be sealed for one hundred years. I cannot know you, who read it now, nor what perils you face. But I ask you to imagine us, so long ago, faced with this bizarre dilemma: what if it were possible to accomplish the slow, secret stealing of the lifeblood of a nation; the delicate, sinister diminishing of its vitality?

This was the threat brought to my friend, the savant Prince Zaleski, in the darkened upper chamber of the decayed palace. Here he had sought solitude to pursue his arcane philosophy, and meditate upon the many curious encounters of his years of wanderings in the East, after his fall from favour at the Court of his youth.

Our visitor, Corstang, was a young man, esteemed in the counsels of state, but showing in his drawn, pale face and tautened brow, a high anguish.

"I come to you, sir, on a matter of the gravest national and I may even say international importance. Lord Grey personally requests that you render the government, the crown, indeed the Empire, your assistance."

Zaleski puffed at his glinting, gem-encrusted narghyle and indicated by the merest slight incline of his head that he was listening.

"Matters stand thus. We are about to conclude a treaty with Russia that will put to an end the decades of rivalry between us in the great expanses of Asia. The Foreign Secretary regards it as of the utmost significance. Further, due to His Majesty's own efforts, we are also in a position at last to find an ally in France. We three Powers together will secure worldwide peace and prosperity for decades to come. But—there is one powder keg primed, and ready to blow all that away at once."

My friend drew his lips from the amber mouthpiece.

"China," he whispered.

"Precisely. Oh, all our influences are quite agreed. Russia undertakes to take no part against us in India, Afghanistan, or the Himalayas. We for our part will not interfere in Mongolia, the Khanate of Bokhara, the Caspian, and the steppes. And neither of us will occupy any part of China, except our existing concessions. This is all clear?"

The Prince flickered an eyelid which the emissary was obliged to take as acquiescence.

"Yet everything would be in jeopardy if we were forced— goaded by some intemperate act of hostility towards us—to take any more active part in China. Russia would suspect us of treachery, France would resent it; all our patient rapprochement would come to nought. Now, the situation in China is fragile. The ancient Dowager Empress cannot live much longer: she may even be secretly dead. Rivals gather to seize the throne. One of them will seek to win power, vying against our interests."

The pale fumes from the scintillant smoking apparatus floated serenely across the chamber.

"Has already done so?" The words came as a gentle murmur. The emissary hesitated.

"Yes."

"In what form?"

"An ultimatum. If we recognise the Mandarin Huan Chi-K'ai as the new Regent, and join him in pursuing all the other Powers from the Celestial Empire, we shall be acknowledged as an ally and given privileges. If we do not—he will strike by stealth against the finest and highest in our nation."

"How?" I demanded.

"He does not say."

"Then it is bluff," I retorted.

"Not so, Shiel," the Prince said, gently. "He has started, Mr. Corstang, has he not?"

The imperial secretary nodded slowly. "But this matter is most confidential—how did you know?"

"By inference. In a matter of mere weeks, no less than fourteen leading figures have removed themselves from their vocation or office—some pleading ill health, others personal reasons, some retiring, some supposedly called to other fields. The reason in each case is tactfully different: the symptoms, I infer, are the same. A Cabinet member, a veteran military man, an eminence in the Church, a philanthropist, even a great investigator, all withdrawn. One, a diplomat who did me a certain service once, even wrote to me in guarded terms. Some influence is working to remove the vigour of these people. I have been brooding upon the matter."

"How could this be the work of the Mandarin?" I demanded.

"That I have not quite yet determined. There are possibilities, however. Let me reflect further."

There was a long silence, broken only by the Prince's indrawings from his great globed smoking-vessel, the fumes agitating and coiling in the precious glass orb. Then, after many moments, the Prince rose, went to his oriental escritoire of inlaid lacquer, and returned, to my immense surprise, to scan the pages of a trivial and jejune society gossip-paper, The Waffler.

At length, Corstang could scarcely control his impatience further. "Sir, you are our final hope. All our discreet investigations have yielded nothing. All around us the great people of our country are relinquishing their duties, going into hiding and refusing to say why. We do not know who will be next. We must not concede to this Mandarin's demands, and yet we cannot let this devilish affair continue. What can we do?"

The Prince stared at his importunate visitor, and smiled delicately. "Do you know anything of fortune-telling?" he enquired.

"F-fortune telling?"

"Yes. I really think you should go and read some teacups."

&

I had always supposed that the collection of ancient relics, curios, talismans, and weird devices kept by my friend the Prince in that one lofty, scented chamber of his old tower must be unrivalled in this country. I was hardly prepared for the rooms kept by Mr. Anstruther Rook, the noted mountaineer and poet, at number 2 Hyde Park Mansions in the city. For some moments after we had entered I was taken aback, and indeed I hardly drew breath. It was as if we had been ushered into an antechamber of the palace of the Caliph Haroun-al-Raschid, preserved by peculiar art and invoked here in London.

The prevailing light was dim, for the windows were veiled in silks, but there was a constant glinting and glimmering from chased silver, ancient gold, glass lamps, from curved weapons, alabaster statuettes, scarlet ushabti, and from a case of Gnostic gems in onyx, carnelian, piccolo, and jet. In one corner stood a piece that might be the sister of the great smoking-vessel in the Prince's chamber: a high narghyle, iridescent with precious stones. Idols, masks, and misshapen heads leered from every wall. From a shining censer there rose faint fumes, tantalising and ethereal in their scent.

The Prince nodded curtly to the young man in his dark velvet jacket, crimson waistcoat, and flowing dark tie, and returned unblinkingly his impudent gaze.

"You have been in China, I perceive."

"Oh, yes, last year. Yunnanfu. It was most instructive."

"Where you met, perhaps, the warlord Huan Chi-K'ai?"

"Perhaps."

"How otherwise could you have obtained the black jade seal upon your fob, which bears (if I am not mistaken) his personal device—the dragon of night, at wing?"

"How indeed?"

"It is given, I believe, only to those who render the Mandarin the most signal service."

Anstruther Rook smiled but gave no reply.

"I read very little modern literature, Mr. Rook. But I could not help sending for your Youth Unbound."

Rook raised an eyebrow. "Splendid. There were only seven sales. It is good to know one of those was to such a connoisseur."

"And another no doubt was to Mrs. Serena Wroxall?"

Rook smirked. "She is indeed a devoted follower of my work, though you would hardly think it of such a stout pillar of commerce. She has a grocer's soul. Still, she keeps me supplied. May I offer you some of her company's excellent Imperial White Tea?"

Prince Zaleski permitted himself a slight smile.

"Thank you, but no. I should not like to deprive you of so rare a thing when supplies may soon become—uncertain."

Our host did not relax the glint in his eyes nor the twist in his lips.

"They were so very dull, Zaleski. All those dreadful statesmen, clerics, orators, pontificators. It has been so blessedly silent without them."

"It cannot be condoned, Rook."

For a moment the poet became almost fierce. "Well, really, Zaleski: why not? These bourgeois devils, these philistines killed Wilde, drove Dowson into poverty, Davidson to suicide, Johnson to drink, Louis Horne to madness. They never do recognise genius or understand the finest edges of discernment, the darkest marges of philosophy. They had to pay, in the subtlest, most artistic way—by becoming like us, weird dreamers!"

My friend held up an elegant hand: and I thought I caught a glimpse, on a pale finger, of a black intaglio ring, but he turned swiftly to depart, and quickly re-donned his delicate lavender gloves. At Rook's outer door, he paused.

"I suggest, sir, you seek those marges elsewhere. That were a better destiny than the life of a white slave, which is what you are rapidly pursuing now. I believe there is much of interest in the coasts of Barbary."

ॐ

Only three indications appeared at the time of the success of my friend's intervention. One was the gradual series of announcements that certain figures had returned, renewed, to public office. Another was a brief trade paragraph stating that Wroxall's Imperial White Tea had been removed from sale, as supplies from the Orient had failed. The third intimated that Mr. Anstruther Rook had gone abroad to pursue his studies into the ecstatic dances of the remote peoples beyond the Rif.

"It was in some measure simple, Shiel," the Prince explained, "once I asked myself, what are the chief imports from China to this country, that is, what tools lay at Huan Chi-K'ai's disposal for him to exert his power here. They are silk, porcelain, orchids, rice and tea. The first three are delicate enough as it is, and tampering with them would be difficult, nor could they easily be used to convey danger to the recipient. Rice would be much easier to contaminate, but it is not consumed in any quantity by sufficient of the class of person the Mandarin wished to affect. Tea, however, ideal: taken almost universally, the very highest teas already known to come from China, and fashionable society is always alert to try out exotic new strains.

"Very well, then. Now I am alert to any unusual changes connected to tea. I scan the papers, which for once I allow to contaminate my refuge here. What do I find? The great tea importer of Wroxall's, whose caddies and caskets grace only the best households, is in disarray. Its head died last year leaving as heir a daughter, Serena, an actress and theosophist, whose ideas—I read in the market pages—are perturbing the company's backers. She is seen, says that charming little tattle-sheet, with a Bohemian crowd—among them, Mr. Anstruther Rook. I have read his book, and see from its fervour and fierceness that here is a man at odds with the world. He is that rare thing: a decadent, yet a man of action. It is likeliest that he, of all her circle, is the key.

"What could have caused such ennui, is plentiful in China, and would bring shame to our great families? Here I surmised: it must be the dragon's seed, a form of opium that may be taken as an infusion. It was introduced into Wroxall's finest Imperial White Tea."

Anstruther Rook seemed to harbour no malice. Often packets of green papyrus would arrive at my friend's ruinous abode, bearing all the aroma of the spices of the Atlas. I recall with what satisfaction the Prince would retire to examine these in his shadowed tower-room, all amongst his other arcane treasures, drawing the while upon the violet fumes from his vast narghyle.

The Return of Kala Persad

I t has been related that I, Kala Persad, met my friend Mark
Poignand in an adventure in India, and came with him
to London in the last years of the old Empress. Here,
Poignand Sahib set up a plaque on his door proclaiming
himself the Manager of a Confidential Advice service: and
people of all castes came to him for help. Secreted in an inner
chamber, I listened to their stories, and was at once able to
know where evil lay: guided by my "intuition", as he called
it, my friend then set out to solve each case by finding proof
that would satisfy the quaint customs of the English courts.

My friend's prowess, however, soon came to the attention
of the Imperial authorities, and he was asked to journey to
the East once more, to help them in a certain delicate matter.
He would have liked me to go with him, but we both knew
I was by then too old for such hardships, and further my
faithful companion, the cobra Kalpa, was also disinclined
to go, as I knew when I consulted him. Dear Poignand used
to describe me as a "snake charmer", a delightful phrase but
one which, alas, betrayed no depth of understanding of the
sacred bond that may exist between man and beast, both of
whom are advanced souls. He appreciated, at least, what he
dimly understood to be my "serpent wisdom", the gift of my
family's ancient knowledge of the ways of the snake.

Thus, I was left alone in the great city, and our parting
was sore, for I could not be sure I should ever see my friend
again, both by reason of the dangers he might face, and my

own advanced age. And still to this day, he has not returned, while I am longer in years, and there is now a King upon the throne. Well was it observed, in the tales told of our exploits, that I am—what was it?—a little, worn, old man, with silver stubble and many crow's feet upon my skin. This I confess to be true. But in other matters, I was amused by what was told of me. I was pictured, I recall, lolling about all day on a charpoy, a woven bed rescued from an East End opium den, or warming my limbs by the fire. Ah, Poignand Sahib, that even such friends as we should so misunderstand each other. When he would find me reclining idly, as he supposed, I was in fact transfixed in meditation, training my mind to that acute level of discernment which enabled me to solve his cases for him in a moment. And when I huddled close to the flames, it was not because I was cold, since I have long mastered matters of the body, but to sharpen my spirit by observing the golden dance of Agni, the fire-god.

It was my habit to give my friend advice on his investigations in brief, terse phrases, so as not to expend my inner energy on trivia: this the dear man mistook for a lack of proficiency in his tongue. But as this narrative will show, I had quite mastered his language. My friend had left me means to sustain myself well enough in my frugal way in his absence, so I did not need money. But his clients still came to him for aid, and were disappointed to find him gone. Sometimes, therefore, I offered my own gentle assistance, but this they mostly declined; some with a delicate courtesy, others rather abruptly. I do not reproach them: how could they know it had always been I, and not solely my friend, who had looked into the darkened ways and seen where the light glinted?

Nevertheless, there were some few who were willing to consider that I, Kala Persad, and my cobra Kalpa, might be of assistance to them. And, further, I decided to keep my wits keen by conducting certain investigations of my own: for he who walks around London with an opened inner eye may soon see mysteries enough. If I am frank, the cases brought to my friend had rarely been of great moment; they were usually quite simple, and rather sordid. They concerned human ambitions: greed, lust, revenge. I found them tiresome. Surely, I thought, there must be stranger and more lofty matters to investigate in this wan land? It was but a small step to decide also that I would myself chronicle these rarer episodes.

It will not be surprising to learn that when I first came to London, I could not eat the same gross food, principally the flesh of beasts, as my dear friend. He put himself out to find a better way for me, and learned that there was, in a quiet back street, a vegetarian café where the few moderately enlightened souls in this vast metropolis could dine on proper food. Here I began to take myself once or twice a day, for my needs are few, and here I have on occasion met others from my own faith, and some interesting Occidentals too. And it was this place that was the occasion of my first true case, discounting those in which I merely advised Poignand on transient mortal affairs. Know then, that it was my habit to take Kalpa with me to this café, not for the food (which he would not enjoy) but to keep me company. My cobra would sleep quite contentedly in a basket I carried.

As I sat enjoying my dhal and salad, a young man entered. He wore a white summer suit, somewhat the worse for wear, and a battered straw hat, from which stuck out fair hair of almost the same colour and texture as the straw. I saw him look anxiously about, with pale blue eyes, which were of the same light I have seen in winter skies. He hesitated, but at last subsided into a chair by a table in a dim corner of the café, still looking about him. My dear friend Poignand has often remarked how I was able to discern the innermost thoughts of men, as if this were some piece of sorcery. It is nothing of the sort. A restless man of action, such as he, does not take the time to contemplate the faces of those he meets, or to observe their little secret movements. Only because of my age, and my years of mental training, am I able to see into hearts. And it was perfectly clear to me that this young, yellow-haired gentleman in the café was carrying a trouble, and had hoped to find here one who would help him.

It happened that at this moment I heard Kalpa stir in his basket. I lifted the lid, and gently raised his hooded head. His eyes, however, were still withdrawn, his thoughts far away in the distant aeons. There had been only some slight flicker in his limbs, perhaps as he recognised himself in a past reincarnation. I replaced him tenderly. Most of the other customers had grown used to my habits by now, and were not in the least perturbed by the sight of Kalpa. But it was not so with the young man. He rose up from his chair, and stared at me in awed fright, until the serpent was restored to his mystic slumbers. Then, hesitantly, the youth advanced towards me, and I beckoned him to be seated at my table. Not every one of his countrymen would consent to be seen with me, I had noticed: but he did not demur. I gazed at him. My eyes have been described as deep and brown, like the waters of the holy river. In truth, they have as many colours as the opal, when I wish. But if I am seeking to offer solace or wisdom, I naturally settle my mind to a state of calm reflection, and it is perhaps this that emanates from my stare. The young man became restless.

"Forgive me," he said, "I had hoped to find a friend here."

"You have done so," I replied.

"I did not mean to intrude upon you. But when I saw you with, with . . . "

"With my companion, Kalpa," I supplied.

"The cobra?"

I nodded.

"You know something about their ways?"

"I am from many generations of what you call *snake-charmers*, yes."

The boy sensed a little haughtiness in my tone.

"Oh, I did not mean to offend you," he said, hastily.

"Look into my eyes," I replied: and for a while I regarded his pale irises and the dark discs of his pupils. Within their sombre gleam, I thought I could discern a slow coiling. I drew back, considering with care what I had seen there. I must proceed cautiously.

"Tell me your trouble," I said, simply.

"I am Peter Revery," he began, as if he were reciting a lesson, "and I am not long down from college. A few months ago, I heard that my uncle, Charles Revery, an old East India man, had died out there, leaving me a fair income and all his possessions. These arrived in tea chests last week, and I have been emptying them one by one to look at their contents. I knew my uncle was a great collector of curios, but had no idea how much he had amassed, nor how very strange some of it was. Some of them bear tickets, with brief explanations of their nature and provenance, but others do not. I have taken a small villa in Hertfordshire while I think what I wish to do, and to house my uncle's things for the time being. I do not think Uncle Charles really knew what it was he accumulated, he was simply attracted by what he saw as the outré and grotesque. I am afraid, too, that from what my late father said, my uncle was not always fastidious about how he acquired these, these—idols."

"Devas," I could not resist correcting him, "Spirits, or gods, if you prefer."

Revery nodded slowly, as if recognising a word he should have known.

"What did you study at your university?" I asked.

"Oriental languages," he said, "at the urging of my uncle. I did not wish to offend him, so I agreed."

"And you are proficient?"

"I would be better if I knew what to do with them. My health is too indifferent for me to follow my uncle's trail to the East. . . Sir, I admit I have always been a dreamer," he continued, in a lower tone, almost a murmur, "and if it had not been for my uncle's legacy, I do not know how I should ever have made my way in the world. As it is, I feel that I must somehow honour the study of the tongues, and the objects that he entrusted to me, and yet I feel ill at ease with them."

"With certain ones in particular?" I asked.

He hesitated.

"Yes. I find myself constantly drawn to a pair of iron candlesticks in the form of the cobra. They are of no very great art or value, I am sure, which is perhaps why they have no tag attached. The metal is dense, the craft is quite crude, and yet I cannot help but look at them. A few nights ago, I placed candles in the sockets, and lit them. It was as if the iron was at once transformed. It—it seemed to remember the fire of the forge. There was a glow inside the hoods, and the heart of the wick seemed to possess a strange glint. And I—I must have raised something, for recently my dreams have begun to take a most troubling form . . . "

At my feet, I felt, rather than heard, a further stirring from the sleeping snake.

"Let us not talk further here," I said, "I will take you to a more appropriate place."

All unknown to the many thousands who mill around the streets of the metropolis, there are a few curious corners of the city which receive only a few chosen visitors. One of these appears to be simply a modest bungalow at the end of a quiet mews, and fronted by a long, rather stark garden of cypresses and urns. Anyone who proceeds to the door (but few do) will notice a plaque reading "Anglo-Pali Translation Service", and inside they will find an office, with many faded pamphlets and gathered sheets of paper, wooden pigeonholes and, at a battered old bureau, an Indian clerk, who will engage them in conversation about the ostensible business carried on here.

There are those, however, who simply nod to the clerk, and go on through an unremarkable door to a corridor leading to the back of the bungalow. Here, a right turn will take them into a bare room furnished only with a few rugs and tambours, and with glass lamps, unusually unlit, resting in little niches. But a left turn will usher them into a room as rich and refulgent as the other is bare, and with an air redolent of sandalwood, jasmine and rose. This is a temple for the people of my faith. However, it was to the room on the right that I first took young Peter Revery, setting Kalpa down in his basket by my side. On our way through the office, I noticed him glancing with curiosity at the papers strewn about.

When we were settled, I said: "Tell me about your dreams."

The youth swallowed, and hesitated.

"I cannot help you unless you tell me all," I urged.

"At first, I am surrounded by blackness", he began. "I do not mean just the dark. Something utterly black, sharp and hard: the white of ice, reversed, if you understand me. And I am no more than a pinprick, a speck of dust. All my awareness of my self seems to be diminished to a very tiny point. And then, very slowly, over and over, shapes begin to form in the black void. At first there is just a glint of light, like a struck flint. And then a dark gleaming radiates from the light, so that I see circles form. The circles begin to move, in great slow coils. The point of light rises up from the coiling forms, up and up. I am no more than a stare: all my attention is fixed upon the forms I see. And then, then . . . "

"Go on," I urged.

"I am plunged into nightmare," he said, simply, but with a terrible weariness, "I am in a vast pit of snakes, of hooded serpents: the circles have become their writhing bodies, the point of light has become their eyes, their many eyes. For hours, as it seems in my dreams, I am at their mercy, as they watch me, ready to make me their prey whenever they might wish. At each moment, I think they might strike, and I am kept on a desperate edge of dread. I do not know why they are waiting, what cruel fascination keeps them watching me, and coiling around me . . . "

I had heard enough to confirm my suspicions. There was little doubt in my mind that Peter Revery had been brought to me, that our fates had been interwoven across the aeons. One thing more was needed, however. I gently raised the lid of Kalpa's basket., and whispered within. I saw the boy draw back.

"Do not be afraid," I said. "Overcome your fear."

The hooded head of the old cobra rose from its straw lair, and swayed. I saw his glittering black eyes regarding the pale youth by my side. The billowing golden neck began to shrink back, as if preparing to strike.

"Hold still," I ordered the young man.

And then the serpent rose up, extending its great muscles as far as they might go, a column of gleaming scales, and very slowly dipped its head. There was an instant in which the room seemed to flicker, as quickly as a snake's tongue, and the bare walls were like tongues of fire: but in less than a breath this subsided, and my companion, the cobra Kalpa receded slowly into his sleeping chamber, upon the silk shawl in the depths of the basket. Then I knew for certain.

"Come with me," I said, and the trembling boy, whose eyes held a mingling of fear and fascination, followed me without words. We entered the temple in the room opposite. The light sparked from the many silver vessels, and shimmered in the hanging veils: violet fumes rose in delicate curls from the incense holders; from around the walls, painted figures with almondine eyes regarded us gravely. I drew Revery aside to a recess in a far wall: here, a sheer veil of silver silk admitted us as if we stepped through mist. Before us was a painted panel, and I felt the boy draw back, startled.

"It is the repose of Lord Vishnu," I said, "The Eternal."

It was not a very good image, if I am frank. There are few of us in London, and we have no wealth. We could not afford one of the Master Painters. And yet it was clear enough for Revery to see. The god was lying upon the ocean of all things, surrounded by hooded snakes, which might be thought of as potentialities. A lotus was about to form before him. To dream, as the young man had done, of this most sacred scene, of the beginning of everything, far, far distant in space and in time, was a sign of the highest importance. Certainly, he and I had been drawn together, through measureless strands of destiny. How else would a worn old *snake-charmer*, and this delicate English boy, be brought together? I explained the matter in as few and as simple words as I could, and was gratified to see the dawning of a new light in his eyes.

"You wanted to know," I said, "what you should do with the tongues you have learnt, and the objects your uncle has gathered. He may not know what he did, but I tell you he was moved by greater forces than the collecting spirit and the nostalgia of the old Indian official. You are a servant of Vishnu, my child, called through the gulfs of the ages. Put your skills to the translating of the sacred texts here, and offer gifts, if you will, from your uncle's hoard to our temple. But those, I think, will be the least of your destiny. The gods of time, of making, of destroying, of preserving, are beginning to waken in London, and we three have much work to do."

Peter Revery breathed deeply of the spiced air. The silver veils stirred from some unseen breeze.

"Three?" he asked, quietly, but I think he knew the answer.

"Yes," I said, "for certainly Kalpa recognised you as an old friend."

Four Curious Books

The 1909 Proserpine Prize

When Mr. Basil Lamport, sole proprietor of the Luminous Gamp Company, a very thriving concern, passed away at the turn of the century, he left a somewhat surprising stipulation in his will. He bade his trustees to set up an annual award, starting at several hundred pounds, for the finest full length work of fiction in a certain tradition in literature. It was his aim to reward the author of the book that most skilfully went into the dark and emerged with something of the light, and so he had named this the Proserpine Prize. In doing so, shrewd merchant that he was, he did not overlook the opportunity this would present his heirs to trade on the particular quality of his famous phosphorescent umbrellas, which aided the foot passenger in the dingy, ill-lit streets from being the prey of any hurtling cab or cart. This very proper commercial consideration aside, though, he averred in the codicil establishing the prize that he did so out of affection for the remarkable works of Lord Lytton, which had accorded him the keenest pleasure in his youth.

I dare say this was the first book prize of any consequence, not counting the very high-minded poetry trophies such as the Newdigate and so forth, handed out by the universities, and it caught the popular imagination, and did no harm at all to the sales of the chosen title. I had the honour to be its secretary from the inception, in 1901, until—well, that will follow—and so was involved in selecting the judges, guiding their reading, and helping them—I trust, with tact—to reach their conclusion.

If I am candid, I ought to say I only achieved the post through the urging of Mr. Lamport's nephew, the residuary legatee. I had known Hugh well at college, we were fast friends until I was sent down: and he knew I was at a loose end and not entirely unlearned in the literature at issue; for old Lamport had infected both of us with the same taste. I almost wondered sometimes if the whole thing were not some elaborate scheme of his shrewd uncle to keep me in moderate means (rather too moderate for my tastes) and out of mischief. It would be like him. For he saw that Hugh was quite out of his wits with worry when, petulantly I admit, I decided to punish the university for banishing me on account of my versions of Verlaine (somewhat free, it must be said) by going out in quest of the tracks of the mad boy poet Rimbaud, among the dregs of Djibouti. Upon my return, malarial and maundering, Hugh saw I was nursed well, through all my fever and delirium: and shortly after this, the secretarial posting came my way.

Yet I believe the record of the prize will commend itself to any discerning reader of the field. It is true that our task was often made simple for us. In the first year, Mr. Shiel's vast epic of the end of the world swept all before it, and in the following year, Mr. Conan Doyle's much-admired detective found himself confronted with that notorious black hound; while in the third year it was impossible to ignore the impact of Mr. Guy Thorne's shocking romance in which faith in the Resurrection is for a while challenged by hoaxed evidence to the contrary.

The procedure decreed by Mr. Lamport was that the judges should convene on the longest night of the year, the 20th December, for their deliberations, so affording them the fullest retrospect of the year that had passed: it was fitting also, of course, for its deep hours of darkness. On these occasions, they first enjoyed a very good dinner at one of the remoter of his former homes, and did not allow their deliberations to interfere with their digestion, or the accompanying libations. After this, they gathered in Lamport's old library and, by fireglow and candlelight (for there was as yet no gas), discussed their choice. I had secured for the year of 1909 the services of three quite public figures (it helped to sustain interest in the prize if the judges were known to the news-sheet readers). The Reverend Mr. Prendergast was a controversial and outspoken parson; Major Fargrave was fresh from his keenly-followed tomb- and temple-digging explorations in Mesopotamia; while Dr. Cornelius Payne of Cambridge, a fashionable lecturer, had lately published an illuminating study of the satires of Macrobius. They were all to be well rewarded, for the solicitors' stewardship of the funds had prospered (which was more than can be said for Hugh's handling of his share), and indeed the prize itself was now worth well over a thousand.

I had beforehand helped them all, in correspondence, to whittle down the titles for debate to seven. In truth, the choice was mostly mine, and they did not demur from it, despite a query as to whether we must admit Miss Barclay's much-discussed *The Rosary*—which, however, I convinced them was not, for all its merits, of the Lyttonian tradition that Mr. Lamport had in view.

I shall list those seven here, so the reader will see how severe was our task in bestowing this ninth annual prize. They was *Jimbo* by Mr. Algernon Blackwood; *Lord Alistair's Rebellion* by Mr. Allen Upward; *Black Magic* by Miss Marjorie Bowen; *The Ghost Pirates* by Mr. William Hope Hodgson; *The Lady of the Shroud* by Mr. Bram Stoker; *Asmat; or, The Secret Names* by "Sabazeus"; and *The Isle of Lies* by Mr. M.P. Shiel.

I thought I could foresee how the drift of the debate might go. It was important to anticipate this. I sensed there was a

49

certain unspoken prejudice against giving the prize to an author twice, and while the vigour and power of Mr. Shiel's new book was undeniable, it was not so clearly in the tradition that our founder wished to honour. While Mr. Upward had recounted a very curious conspiracy, somewhat in the vein of Mr. Shiel and Mr. Thorne, I did not think it had quite the glamour or gusto of their winning works. I thought there might also be a certain reluctance to award the laurels to a pseudonymous work, and that it might be considered that, powerful as I certainly thought it was, it rendered the dark too well and the light very weakly. The converse was true of Mr. Blackwood's book. Warmth for him would, I felt, be great: but *Jimbo*, for all its charm and fancy, was not, I thought from the shadiest side of his palette, nor quite of the stature we sought.

On the other hand, there would be a decided willingness to honour the author of the immortal *Dracula*, even if for a lesser work; there would be a boldness in giving Miss Bowen, as a woman and a first author, the prize; and, perhaps most of all, there might be a swell of opinion that thought Mr. Hodgson unjustly thwarted the previous year when his remarkable story of a haunted house in Ireland was swept away by Mr. Chesterton's extraordinarily vivid nightmare of anarchists and paradoxes.

All of this, by way of preamble to an account, these many years after the event, which I have no doubt could be attributed by the sceptic to the richness of the late Mr. Lamport's cellar, or to the ripe Stilton that accompanied its offerings. I will assert that no such cause was responsible, and describe as minutely and carefully as I may what transpired that winter solstice night during the judging of the 1909 Proserpine Prize—which I suspect those present, good men though they were, hope never to see again, nor anything remotely approximating it, as long as their days shall last.

It was bitterly cold without and we were glad of the well-kindled fire in its huge hearth and the great golden stone walls of our patron's retreat in Dassett Magna, in the heart of the shires not so distant from Oxford. A portrait of Mr. Lamport, with his fair, well-combed hair, weeping-willow moustache, ruddy cheeks and kind, if (I often thought) rather tired eyes, gazed benevolently over our preparations. I spread out the seven books, sent by their publishers for the occasion, upon the walnut table, and my three Magi regarded them. Candles in their glinting silver sticks cast a bright glow, or a pool of shadow, upon the bindings. I remember noticing that Mr. Hodgson's pirates and Mr. Stoker's pale lady flared out in the flickering light, while Mr Blackwood's winged boy sheltered half in shade, and the book of "Sabazeus", at the end of the arc, was quite hidden in gloom.

The house lay in the lea of a little range of rounded hills and on the top of one of these some 16th century squire had set up a conical beacon tower, crowned with a gaunt black iron cresset. He said it was to warn of the coming of the Spanish, but the credulous peasants counted him a warlock who meant to use it for certain secret fermentations, and kept their children (or those they could not spare) close by them. A pair of great glazed doors at the bay of the library led out into modest grounds and gave a prospect of this edifice. I shared this pleasing folk tale with my three guests, who merely nodded at me vaguely.

On one of the bookcases I had ranged, as had become the custom, the past winners of the award, now eight in number, in case the panel wished to consult the verdict of previous years and compare it with their own. Their vari-coloured spines, in gilt on scarlet or black or royal blue, rested in triumphant state.

I diffidently suggested we might begin. Mr. Prendergast adjusted his round spectacles upon a narrow nose. "For my part, gentlemen," he began, "I own to being very attracted by both Mr. Blackwood's delicate tale, and Mr. Upward's very correct warning against the forces of reaction in our society—ritualists, sensualists, malcontents, and suchlike. Either of those would win my favour."

Major Fargrave caressed his admirable red beard. "Hmm, see what you say, padre. But speaking as a man who has seen a bit of action in his day, that fellow Shiel has got it for me. No ninnying about with him. And if not him, and I admit he's had it once already, I rather fancy this Miss Bowen." There was a slight pause, broken by the crackling of the flames. "Her book, I mean, is striking, very. Lots of colour and incident."

Dr. Cornelius Payne played with a scarlet intaglio ring upon the little finger of his left hand, smiling secretly to himself. "Then we are quite divided it seems. For, with regard to literary distinction in the Gothic tradition, which is what—I fancy—we are seeking, there is no doubt that it is Messrs. Hodgson and Stoker who are in the van."

The vicar tittered and the military man grunted appreciatively, and there was a chorus of "who would have thought it", "dear, oh dear", and "a pretty pass".

I allowed this to subside.

"May I suggest a protocol, gentlemen? You have each attached importance to two of the titles before us. Let me suggest that you now choose just one of those as being the book you most wish to advance, and that you speak at a little more length upon each of them. Then we shall see whether any of you can be persuaded to come round to the other's view."

There was general assent to this proposition, although Dr. Payne still calmly averred that his two were worth more than all the others. I suggested a short time for reflection upon their choice, fortified by another round of the crystal decanters, and they each fingered and flicked through the titles ranged upon the table, shunning though the mustardy binding of the book called *Asmat*.

This scheme did not work as I had suggested it might. When the Reverend Mr. Prendergast said he would have to opt for Allen Upward's *Lord Alistair's Rebellion*, evidencing its penetrating analysis of sin masquerading as beauty, Dr. Payne said his own inclinations of the two were more toward the evident distinction of Mr. Blackwood. Upon the Major proclaiming that they really ought to take the dive and give the prize to a woman, and a younger author at that, Mr. Prendergast said he could not countenance proclaiming a book that exhibited far too evident a glee in sorcery and made Antichrist seem vested in glamour. Dr. Payne's reluctant concession that he would proffer the claims of Stoker above those of Hodgson drew a rebuttal from Major Fargrave to the effect that there was a good deal more to be said for the raw courage of the mariners in the latter's tale. So far from breaking the stalemate, I appeared to have redoubled it. The three judges sat in silence a while, as the fire spat and faltered somewhat, and the chill from outside seemed to emanate into the room.

I ventured another, though perhaps not very laudable, route out of the impasse. "There is the seventh book, of course, which we have not touched on as yet: *Asmat*."

"Oh, that," said Dr. Payne, adjusting his cravat of peacock-blue. "Very curious, certainly. If we knew more of the author . . . "

"Whoever wrote it knows a thing or two," conceded Fargrave, wagging his coppery beard. "What he says of the phylacteries and talismans of the Near East is quite spot on. I've seen some of them, and what they mean out there . . . "

"There is a certain amount of learning in it as to the pseudepigrapha too," the parson observed, fingering his spectacles, "though the book is very heterodox and scarcely edifying. Too much hocus-pocus about the secret names of lost gods and suchlike. And a very disreputable publisher—Smithers, wasn't it?"

This last remark seemed to commend the title to the other two judges somewhat more, and I saw them exchange glances. I took up the volume where it lay in shadow, and contemplated its yellowy cloth and black titles. But none of the judges reached out for it, so I replaced it softly. It fell open upon the front endpapers. An inscription had been made there, in deep ink, and not obviously in the Roman alphabet. It was in three separate passages and the characters in each differed. One might at first think this was some publisher's decoration meant to draw the reader in with quaint hieroglyphs, but it was too artfully done for that: the impress and the richness of the figuring showed it was made by hand, not press.

"Here, what do you make of this?" I said, setting aside for the moment my duty to bring the matter of the prize to a conclusion.

Fargrave looked up, caught by my tone, and came around to peer over my shoulder. Then he whistled and pointed a lean, bronzed finger at the topmost passage: "Chaldean, or I'm an apeman," he murmured, and he took the book up and glared at the arcane symbols, "But in a very early form, hard to make out. Who the devil—" He glared at me, and I shrugged. "And the others?" I asked. He was still trying to decipher the first phrase, his dry lips working away. "Eh? Oh, nearer home. Classical stuff I expect. But this . . . "

His interest had by now sufficiently piqued the curiosity of his fellow judges. Dr. Payne gently guided the major's hands so that they replaced the book on the table. Then he moved both the silver candlesticks so that they cast a full light upon the manuscript endpaper. I saw him raise a single faint smudge of tawny eyebrow. "This third passage," he remarked, "was evidently meant for me. Why? Because it is in Macrobian Latin. Some of that great satirist's works were too treacherous or too—hmm, fleshly—for his time. So he devised a cipher, itself written in private sigils: like this. There can be scarcely six or seven scholars in the world who know enough of it."

"Name them, then," observed the churchman, "and we should all be a good deal nearer knowing the authorship of this book." Dr. Payne became thoughtful, and started muttering, ticking off his fingers: "Aldard of Caius, too dull; Anstruther Rook, no doubt, could certainly be him; Wherwell, that old hermit, won't be him; the Venetian Baron, maybe; that young French prodigy . . . " I took the book gently from him, as I could see the third of the party was anxious to have his say.

Mr. Prendergast cast his glance upon the open page and peered at the characters. After a few moments he looked up quickly. "I see," he said. "You, Major, know this first set here as Old Chaldean; whereas you, Doctor, know the third set as Macrobian Latin." They both nodded, though deep in their own thoughts. "Well, then, the second set is clearly meant for me. Unless of course, you, Mr. Secretary, are versed in strange tongues?"

I laughed, and shrugged. "You are the judge, sir," I said.

"Mmmm. You will all think it odd, no doubt, that a churchman of my advanced views—oh, I know what people say—should have an interest too in the ancient. But I do, and for a very good scientific reason. I want people to get as close as possible to the original meaning of our sacred texts, without the accretions of the ages: to the very purest form of our faith. And that is why, in my way, I am an amateur of Coptic. And this second passage is written in Church Coptic, but abstrusely and with certain terms I cannot at first fathom out. Well, well, whoever did all this certainly knew how to engage our interest in the book. It somehow seems an unfair advantage. Can we admit it, I wonder?"

He looked at me. "I think I may fairly say there is nothing in Mr. Lamport's codicil touching on the matter," I replied.

"Very remiss of Mr. Lamport," remarked the cleric dryly, nodding up at the portrait of our benefactor.

I allowed a further silence to lapse while they each contemplated the texts of their specialism. Fargrave waved his glass at me and I replenished each in turn, feeling somewhat more the valet rather than the valued literary secretary. I decided it was time to move things along.

"This is all very engrossing, I do not doubt, but I must remind you of the need to reach a decision on the prize. Do you feel any nearer to a view, gentlemen?"

They all looked at me in astonishment. The major burst out: "Oh, give it to . . . " He cast his gaze over the titles spread before him, alighted on one and with a wave of the hand said . . . "Stoker and have done."

"Yes," murmured the young divine, "Stoker would do very well. Manly, romantic, innocent, just the stuff—I believe they say." Dr. Payne regarded me steadily. "There we are then. Very easily resolved. Now"—turning to his companions—"suppose we take it in turns to examine *this* more thoroughly, copy out 'our' passages, and mull them over?"

I looked at them quite aghast. "Surely this will not do," I returned, "you have scarcely considered all of the books properly at all."

They quite ignored me. I took a candle from the mantelshelf, went to the window and rubbed moisture from its long panes, with a sweeping gesture of my arm. The silence in the room as the thoughtful savants wrestled with the mysteries before them deepened as the night deepened. I went towards the great hearth fire and gave the smouldering log a kick, then attacked the coals savagely with the bronze poker. The flames leapt into life and their tongues of shadow played upon the lined visage and glinting beard of Major Fargrave. "Syllables, stem words, the sense of a meaning yet no meaning I know," he rumbled. The parson was looking down at some scribbled pencil notes. "Yes, I am in the same case: I have seen some such terms as these in the marginalia of certain Syrian muniments and in the angel-lists of remote Judean hermitages, yet they do not quite cohere into a form I can recognise." Dr. Cornelius Payne inspected his agate fob jewel with care. "This is no Macrobian formulation that I know of," he at length declared. "Yet I feel if I were to make some sort of sideways lunge at it, I might have it in my grasp." I allowed a few more brittle moments to relapse.

"Why don't you try reading them aloud, each in turn?" I suggested. "Something may leap out at you then."

"Most sensible thing you've said all evening, boy," the major growled, and the others nodded. "Can't do any harm," muttered Payne, wearily.

Major Fargrave began. Carefully, a little falteringly at first, he enunciated the Old Chaldean formulation before him. It sounded harsh and barbarous in the somnolence of the library. Then he seemed to gain in confidence and his crooked white teeth shone in his great red beard as he uttered the phrases with more vigour and his jaws worked almost as if independently of his will. The others watched him quite transfixed, but I, from the corner of my eye, saw the pages of the copy of *Asmat* upon the walnut table stir somewhat. There may have been a draught. The major completed his brief recital but his eyes stayed staring in front of him while his jaw continued to work silently as if reaching for words it could not find.

The Reverend Mr. Prendergast stood up and glanced down at his notes. His glasses caught the scarlet and gold of the blazing fire. His thin lips hissed, as if unwillingly, a sequence of strange syllables, then the words stumbled out in a vast torrent while he swayed from side to side and seemed almost to genuflect at certain phrases, with a swift dip of his shiny head. As he did so, I saw that the leaves of the seventh book flickered in sympathy. I heard that ao, ael, ao, ael recurred in all the words he chanted, until he too stopped abruptly, or stopped in sound, for his lips still moved.

Dr. Payne seemed supine, with his eyes closed. Then he started a soft moaning in which the most curious contortions of words I half-remembered from my youthful classics lessons could dimly be discerned. The drone rose and fell from his fleshy pouting mouth, gathering pace, until it became a veritable hail of the most insistent gibberish. He accompanied this with gesticulations of his gemmed fist and, perhaps because of the vigorous vibrations in the air that resulted, the book attributed to Sabazeus jumped upon the table as if in glee. It landed with a vast echoing crash that brought a halt to the doctor's utterances, and drew the eyes of all three of my—"Magi"—towards it.

Then the book began to speak. Its yellowy jaws, like ancient flesh too long entombed, gaped open and its many white tongues flickered rapidly, rapidly like wild creatures who lap when they are athirst, and from each came words and words and words, all outlandish to human ears, some in a strange slow groaning, some in a shiver of sounds like the susurrus of the sea on the sand, some in a gnarled knotty grating like the twisted limbs of trees in a storm, some like the scutter of dead leaves in autumn or the turning of parchment in a vast vellum volume, and some like the crackling of flames.

Then I remembered the flames, and turned and scattered a little powder over the hearth-fire. It roared up with a weird white glow and in it my three wise men stood pale and agape, and I laughed. "Quickly!" I said, and ushered them to the paned door, "Get out of this." They allowed themselves to be led to the stone steps descending into the blessedly silent garden. And as they did so, the deep darkness without was burst asunder by a vast crown of fire, like a door opening upon Gehenna. The cresset was alight. Feverishly, tripping over one another, they drew back into the room, and Dr. Payne squeaked "The warlock! The warlock!" Yet things were no better inside. Upon the table, below the white candles, all oblivious of its six rivals, the book called *Asmat* did not abate in its ululations. For a moment, each man tensed as if to make a movement towards it, but at the merest, slightest movement of their bodies, its chantings rose up a pitch and it seemed to gather a fierceness and fury about it. I edged around it and, while seemingly eyeing up what I might do, I threw behind me some more of Mr. Lamport's most useful compound of phosphor powder upon the fire. It ignited with a roar and a hard white glare. This proved enough. Faced with the devil within or the distant magician without, the three judges of the 1909 Proserpine Prize for Lyttonian literature fled precipitously through the garden doors. I strolled after them and, in the vast golden glow of the village of Dassett Magna's customary midnight winter solstice celebrations, saw their shadowy forms, limned with uncanny light, flee out of the grounds, through or over the lodge gates and out upon the road to the station, merely some three miles distant.

I turned to my book, still pronouncing to itself upon the table. I called to mind the words of banishment from Rimbaud's grimoire and uttered them. Its white tongues flapped for a bit, as if they had much more to say and were not quite willing to obey, then they faltered to a halt.

When Hugh came in after fulfilling his squirely duties as master of ceremonies at the cresset, we sat staring together at the now gently purring hearth-fire. He raised a toast, in an unorthodox manner, in his uncle's amber Malmsey: "To *Asmat*," he said, "the undoubted victor in the 1909 Proserprine Prize, with all the lucre that accompanies it. I say—you don't think there's any chance that one of those trio will challenge what you say?"

"Hardly likely," I replied. "What on earth could they say? 'We all thought it was Stoker, but that book told us otherwise?' Oh ho, no. Shouldn't wonder if they claim the credit for their great percipience in backing an outsider: 'The critics may gainsay us, but here was a book that really spoke to us . . . ' " Our laughter rang around the room.

Hugh smirked at Basil Lamport's picture. "And here's another toast, to 'Sabazeus'," he added, winking at me. "And make sure that Smithers hands over the oof to his author when the solicitors send it in his care."

"Oh, I will," I replied. "And here's one more. To Jean-Nicholas Arthur Rimbaud and his lost Red Sea years; to the studies in arcane literatures that he pursued—and I found—among the Abyssinian mages on the shores of Lake Assal; and to the secret names he gave me."

The Late Post

Hubert Essendine always regarded it as in the nature of an affront when he did not receive any post at all on any one of the days when it is normally delivered. For one thing, he belonged to so many learned, and some unlearned, societies, that he expected to receive the journals or newsletters or miscellaneous correspondence of at least one of these each day, whether the subject was lighthouses, parcel tickets, imperial exhibitions, matchbox labels, the byways of literature, yew trees or the feeding of peacocks, all of which had interested him, and in moments continued to interest him. And for another, he was a voracious purchaser of books, and expected to receive a satisfyingly rectangular brown-paper parcel, indicative of bibliographic content, on almost every delivery day, even if many of the contents remained unread for quite some time.

He was upstairs in his study when he heard the rattle of his letterbox and the scuffle on the doormat which indicated that, on this day at least, he was not to be disappointed. To prolong the anticipation about what might have arrived, he steadfastly completed a passage in his monograph about ships in bottles and then leant back in his creaking wooden chair to review to himself what he had recently ordered. While he was so preoccupied, there was a suggestion at the edge of his hearing of some further rustling in the vicinity of his front door. It sometimes happened that the postman overlooked a letter or two, and returned to add this to his pile, or even that a neighbour received one of his letters by mistake, and obligingly corrected the postman's error for him. Mr. Essendine was always glad when they did so without actually calling at his door: for there was really no need to do so, and it invariably involved a certain amount of idle chatter, which he deprecated, for it kept him from his pursuits. Such a further delivery, anyway, to the extent that he gave it any thought at all, he supposed must have happened, and it was all to the better: it meant there would be even more for him to peruse.

He found, on completing his contemplations, that there were four items he was most anticipating. They were: a Finnish "Jazz" safety match label in red, gold and black, depicting a dancing couple festooned with balloons (he was averse to the supposed "music" they were evidently enjoying, but the label was unusual); a monograph on compassion by the learned Professor Guildea, which he wanted, not for the subject-matter (which did not interest him particularly), but for its rarity; a collection of Wye Valley omnibus tickets, whose destinations (the Golden Valley, Peterchurch, Lyonshall, Hoarwithy) he liked the sound of, but never intended to visit; and a special edition of *The Beast with Five Fingers* by W.F. Harvey, which he had spotted in a most unlikely book catalogue.

It was his principle to ask for dealers to send him catalogues on subjects about which even he was, at present anyway, uninterested. There were two reasons for this: firstly, that he *might* become interested in them; and, secondly, and more importantly, that it was very often possible to pick up titles that did not really belong with the specialism of the dealer, and who did not therefore know very much about them. A dealer in theology, for example, might find himself with a book of ghost stories in a large auction lot, vaguely recognise there was a certain readership for that kind of thing, and mark it up modestly enough, for the alert Mr. Essendine, alone among all those searching for patristic texts or obscure pseudepigraphia, to snap up.

The Harvey he had found in the catalogue of a dealer in books on zoology, taxidermy, bestiaries, and exploration in search of rare or unknown animals. It was plain to see how a book with such a title had been miscategorised by someone in a hurried or idle moment, so that it ended up with the zoological dealer. Without, he supposed, looking at it very much, the slightly exasperated bookseller had evidently put the very modest price upon it and then patiently explained in his annotations to the book that it was not in his normal line but might be of interest to someone, and, furthermore, that he had priced it to sell (a curious expression, as if he priced his other books so that they did not sell, which in fact Essendine suspected some dealers actually did). What the man meant, of course, was "to sell quickly"—he evidently wanted to be rid of this cuckoo in his nest of creatures.

What Essendine knew, but the dealer evidently did not, was that this was a really rather rare edition of Harvey's book. It was true that he already had four other copies of it: the first edition, a later edition, a paperback, and a colonial edition with a different coloured binding: and true, also, that he had never actually fully read any of them, though he had glanced at some of the pleasingly written, if improbable, tales. But he liked the idea of the books, anyway, and was sure that one day, on browsing his shelves, the title would suddenly take hold of him and he would find himself gripped, perhaps even for a whole afternoon.

This particular edition had been issued to "tie-in", as the trade term had it, with a "movie" (another expression he disliked) of the title story, a vulgarity which Essendine rather deplored, still more as it came complete with a coloured strand of paper, in bright colours and with a lurid message, that was looped around the book with the aim of commanding the reader's attention. This was what was known in the trade as a "wraparound band". Very often, and understandably, readers discarded this when they bought the book—it was always slipping off anyway—and so it was unusual to find an intact copy. But that was precisely what Robert Denbigh, the zoological book dealer, was apparently offering. Essendine did not quite rub his hands in that glee which apparently always demands such an activity: but he did permit a satisfied inward smile. His acquisition amply justified his technique of acquiring apparently irrelevant catalogues, and the hours spent scouring them for such oddities.

A further faint rustle in his hallway, no doubt the letters settling down amongst themselves in the disordered array in which they had landed, drew him back to the origin of his very satisfactory reverie. He sprang down the stairs with a light heart, still swiftly speculating on what might have arrived for him. And then he came to a very abrupt and unbelieving halt. For the doormat, with its thicket of tawny bristles, and the hall carpet, with its tired pattern of old roses, were both completely bare. Not a thing was there: not even a bill or circular.

Mr. Essendine was incredulous, and candidly outraged. He lifted up the doormat, he even turned back the carpet, he opened the oak door and looked outside: all to no avail. Baffled and frustrated, he advanced to his gate: there was no sign of the postman, nor of any neighbour or passer-by, nor even of any letters that might have somehow, inexplicably, been swept into the street. He was, in a way, quite relieved not to see the postman, for he would feel obliged to ask him about the matter, and that would result in some conversation, probably involving the postman's views on such matters as the weather, his round, the neighbouring houses and suchlike, none of which were of the remotest interest to Mr. Essendine:

he preferred to keep that necessary official at a distance, so that no future possibility of doorstep dialogues might be encouraged, whenever a parcel was too large for the letterbox.

At last it was borne in upon him that he must have been mistaken, and this, of course, irked him all the more. He spent much of the morning reviewing all the correspondence that he *should* have received, and writing terse, frosty reminders both to the learned societies and to the booksellers whom he regarded as delinquent in this matter. There was a certain satisfaction in that: but it was hardly the same as actually having something to open and enjoy that day.

The days that followed were no better. In fact, they duplicated this first one. He was not at home every time, and when at home he was not always within earshot of the letterbox (he liked not to give way to his morbid need for post too evidently, and so would engage himself sometimes outdoors, with the garden, or the workshop where he made models). But when he was near enough to hear, on each occasion he thought there was what had been the customary rattle and rustle, and even a supplementary rustle: and equally on each occasion, upon his arrival, there was nothing there. He began to doubt for his equanimity. Not for his sanity, for a man (he told himself) with so many absorbing avocations was unlikely ever to lose control of his mind. No matter how frustrating this peculiar matter of the post was, he could always shake it off by intricate work upon a carved walnut-shell boat in his workshop, or by working really hard at his essay upon Edwardian street lamps. However, there was the undeniable fact that many people owed him some post: a letter, a journal, a subscription notice, and of course the several books that he had ordered. To these he sent a second, more peremptory, but also (to the sympathetic reader) more importunate reminder note. He was so much at a loss that he even began to nod to, and briefly converse with, those he saw in the street when he went to the post box. They, for their part, were clearly taken aback by this unexpected interlocution and were only able to murmur the sort of inanities that Mr. Essendine had always previously tried to shun. He bore them as best he could, and they bored him better than they knew.

Some of his correspondents telephoned him (it was an instrument he heartily loathed and usually discouraged), courteously, but also rather curtly, to say that they had indeed despatched the item he expected, which would no doubt be with him shortly: and if not, he might like to enquire of the post office. Mr. Essendine was constitutionally averse to dealing with official bodies, even of so largely benign a nature as the post office, and so put this off for the time being. But of all the things he had ordered, he was naturally the most troubled about the Harvey book, and directed his particularly imploring inquiries about it to the zoological Mr. Denbigh. The latter also made use of the devil's instrument to inform his customer, in a somewhat wary and wan voice, and a distinctly off-hand manner, that he certainly had sent the book to him, and was glad to be rid of it, and it ought to be with him by now. If it hadn't arrived, suggested Mr. Denbigh, then he really ought to go to the sorting office who would surely be able to give him a hand with the problem.

Mr. Essendine did not share the confidence of the dealer in bestiaries in the assistance he was likely to get from the post office, and he somewhat resented Denbigh's attitude: indeed, he strongly felt that he was being palmed off in some way. But there was little more he could say, so he replaced the receiver rather tetchily onto the telephone, on the table where it stood in the hallway, next to the wrought-iron umbrella stand. He was now frankly at a loss and sighed noisily to himself. Suddenly, none of the occupations with which he diverted himself seemed to have any lustre. The painted Chinese tea-chest he was restoring could stay pale and faded; the collection of toll-bridge tickets (Oxen 1d, Asses 2d, Children 3d) could stay unsorted; the discovery of a Roman nettle he had made in his garden could stay unreported to that natural history society; all were dust and ashes to him. A cloud of despondency descended upon him and he felt the need to steady himself. He gripped the edge of the umbrella stand, rattling in their cage the black city umbrella, the green country umbrella, the Malacca cane, and the silver-handled visiting stick he always kept there, but so seldom used: for he hardly ever went to town, or walked in the country, or paid visits; such excursions would, after all, result in him encountering people, and they, even his own very limited acquaintance, were invariably not so interesting as his pursuits—and would only detain him.

Mr. Essendine felt very tired and his eyesight seemed fading. He shook his head and tried to focus a little better. He trained his gaze upon the bookshelf that stood in the hallway. And then he became quickly alert. There was a vividly-coloured spine he did not recognise. Even though he acquired so many books, he hardly ever mistook what he possessed. But this was not a volume of his: or, though, was it? As he advanced towards it, the contents of the umbrella stand rattled back into place. Then he stood still, disbelieving. The legend on the spine of the book told him that this was the W.F. Harvey title he had ordered. There was no doubt about it. It was not the first, later, colonial, or paperback edition: it was the "movie" edition. His first thought was that he must, after all, have received, unwrapped, and shelved the book, and then forgotten all about it. It seemed scarcely possible: and yet it must be so. He felt very sick and weary. He must first telephone Mr. Denbigh and apologise, and explain, or explain if he could: and that would be rather mortifying, hardly to be faced. He had better, anyway, first make sure. He reached towards the book.

The thought struck him then that the coloured publicity strip, the so precious accessory to the book, was missing: or at least, it was not wrapped around the spine as it should be. His temporary regret at wronging Mr. Denbigh by doubting the delivery of the book gave way at once, unreasonably, to annoyance that the book was not "as described". He leant forward abruptly to take out the volume and make sure. As he did so, an outpouring of letters, circulars, and small packets descended in a flickering brown cascade upon him, as if they had been thrust behind all the books on the shelves and kept hidden there. He put the book down, fell to his knees and began to examine them: they included many of those he had been expecting. A great surge of bewilderment swept through him as he crawled about on the floor, picking them up and throwing them down to no real purpose, simply checking and re-checking what he was seeing.

And then he found the very rare Guildea monograph and cursed loudly. Whatever had transpired with the post in his hallway had been particularly hard on this thin paper booklet. It bore all the signs of much fingering, with its pages rubbed, its corners crushed, its very lettering dimmed as if by the constant touch of a too-attentive reader. The whole thing, Essendine thought with disgust, looked positively pawed. He tossed it aside with revulsion, where it fluttered helplessly on the floor for a few moments, and its rustling seemed to echo in the various little nooks and niches of the hall.

He was still struggling to understand quite what could have happened for all his correspondence to have been crumpled behind his books in that way—surely it could not be some practical joke of the postman or a neighbour. True, he hardly knew them enough to judge whether they would play such a trick upon him, but it must be unlikely. People simply didn't; or did they? He reflected, suddenly calm, that he could not know what people did or did not do. They were a world unknown to him.

But his collector's instinct soon reasserted itself. The Guildea monograph was almost ruined, true, but it might be retrievable. What about the Harvey? Why had it arrived, however it had, without the all-important paper blazon? A thought occurred to him, and he went back upstairs to his desk. He brought back with him Robert Denbigh's catalogue and turned the pages abruptly for the entry he wanted. He glared at this and he strode towards the dreadful telephone. And then his whole body shook with a convulsive laughter, which came in great groaning gulps. Anyone chancing to call—but no-one ever did chance to call—would have seen him slumped upon the floor, his flesh racked with a shivering ripple and his face oddly contorted.

There was a really rather amusing misprint in the zoological book catalogue. Instead of stating that the special "movie" edition of W.F. Harvey's *The Beast with Five Fingers* came with a special wraparound band, there was the faintest elision to the bottom curve of the "b" which made it look as if . . . oh dear, oh dear . . . he laughed as if he could not stop.

And then he dimly saw the splayed pages of Professor Guildea's monograph fall back gently into place, to the company of a sound like a persistent patting. Then there was a sudden scurrying noise, but his eyes were blurred with the tears of his laughter, and he could not quite catch sight of whatever had caused it.

As he lay there, still gurgling and shaking to himself, he felt a slight touch upon his face. He moved as if to brush it away, but his limbs were too weak to comply. The touch was followed by another, firmer and more definite, and more, with a swift pattering: and Essendine understood that there were fingertips exploring his brow, temples, cheeks, jaw, lips. He opened his mouth to shout out in protest (though there was no-one who would hear), but the fingers closed around his lips and smothered whatever it was that he might have cried out. Then the fingers began to stroke his face, in long, lingering caresses, and he found he wanted to call out even more, but could not, because all his body was tautened. Still the deplorable, intimate fingers worked slowly and delicately over his face, and Essendine began, despite himself, to feel his flesh thrill to their caress, while his mind roared out an anguished protest. With a great effort of will he made his own hand reach toward the umbrella stand. The hook of the city, or the country, umbrella would do, if only he could reach one, to catch hold, without any need for *him* to touch it, of the thing upon his face, and to fling it across the room. All he had to do was reach out. But even as he formed the thought, he knew that there was a curious irresolution growing within him: that he was not sure if this was what he really wanted.

[With thanks to Richard Dalby, whose description of the film tie-in edition of *The Beast with Five Fingers*, in his introduction to the W.F. Harvey anthology *The Double Eye* (Tartarus Press, 2009) prompted the idea for this story. Its other inspiration, of course, was "How Love Came to Professor Guildea" by Robert Hichens.]

An Incomplete Apocalypse

"I think you make out your case quite well," conceded Burns, leaning back in his crimson leather armchair, "but there's something missing that would really clinch it."

Hugo Winwick gazed across at him with pale, silvery eyes, and made a noise indicative of polite curiosity.

They were discussing his paper on later medieval English apocalypses, submitted to the journal Burns edited, *The Hourglass*. It was a respectable place to be published, and Winwick was quite keen to appear there. In looking at illustrated manuscript volumes of the Revelation of St. John the Divine, he had, some months ago, experienced his own minor revelation. He had begun to speculate that there had been a turning point in the production of these vivid apocalypses, when they were no longer made mainly for *pious* use, but simply as aesthetic objects, as ornamental books. They had moved from the preserve of the abbot, the prior, and the bishop to that of the courtier, even the dilettante. Noble and gentle folk, he contended, had them made simply because they liked looking at fiery monsters. It could be seen, if you liked, as a first surging of the longing for the Gothic in the human spirit: an important new artistic thesis.

Winwick was fairly certain that in his specialist field this was quite a new line to suggest, and he wanted to get his work known soon, in some authoritative venue. Up until then, the assumption had been made that any illuminated and calligraphic text on a biblical theme (and there were hardly any others) had been painstakingly produced by monks in their scriptoria for the edification of zealous patrons, keen to study scripture in handsome volumes. Yet he had found, by a fresh scrutiny of several fragmentary examples, that in later years, just before the dawn of printing, many had been made by skilled, *secular* scribes: artisans, creating their work for worldly and wealthy clients who simply wanted something luxurious and magnificent to feast their eyes upon—and, no doubt, to flaunt at their neighbours and visitors.

"Yes," the editor of *The Hourglass* continued, "what you need to find is an apocalypse completely out of any churchly context. I'm quite persuaded by your line of thought, but in each example you've found, a conventional religious motive *might* still be possible. If you could find and describe one that was bound up only with purely literary or scholarly pages—oh, legends, fabulous histories, almanacs, that kind of thing—your argument would be so much more powerful."

"Yes, I quite see that," his would-be contributor agreed. "And I'm convinced some must exist. But I haven't come across one yet. We'll have to do without. Unless you have any ideas?"

Burns seemed to hesitate, and began to scrape his pipe out with a silver device designed for this purpose. This was evidently a sign that he wanted to think. The scraping marked out the silence like a clock's ticking. At last he paused, and looked at Winwick in a sideways sort of way.

"We-ll. There certainly is a likely contender. The Draycott. Do you know it?"

"The Draycott Apocalypse?" The name murmured at the back of Winwick's mind, though he could not say quite why.

"Yes. Incomplete, of course. But they so often are."

"Pages sold off to collectors by indigent owner?" asked Winwick, to show that he knew the way of these things.

"No doubt."

But the author felt an unusual quiver of frankness pass through him.

"I don't know much about it, I'm afraid," he confessed.

Winwick was hesitant in admitting to this deficiency in his learning to the notoriously severe editor. But to his relief Burns shook his head.

"I'm not at all surprised. It's never been written up. But from what I understand, it's bound up with all sorts of other stuff, not in the least pious. That might be the lead you need."

He agreed, keenly.

"We've had a few chaps in the past offer to do a feature on it, as it happens. I even gave them introductions to the owner. It's supposed to be quite fine, what's left anyway. But for one reason or another, they never did send me a paper. Flighty blighters, I expect, who liked the idea of getting their name in, but couldn't be bothered to put in the fieldwork."

He cocked a sardonic eyebrow, and blew lustily into the pipe bowl, as if scattering such idle defaulters to the winds, with the dead ashes.

Winwick took the hint.

૪૭

Before pursuing the obscure apocalypse further, Hugo elicited from the editor the names of the two young scholars who had each raised with him before the idea of writing an article about it. And then he checked various digests and catalogues to ensure that they had not, in fact, already written up the book in some *other* journal or book, spurning Burns: he would look foolish if he had been forestalled. But there was no sign whatever of any work of this kind; and, indeed, no sign whatever of the supposed authors, so that Winwick began to wonder if the editor of *The Hourglass* might have got their names wrong. However, when he asked amongst some of his academic acquaintances, he found that a few had indeed heard, rather vaguely, of the two young antiquarians, though none recently. Some wondered if they had been lured by American universities.

"Yes, they've probably gone off to the New World," said one, old McGibbon. "Warmer climes and brighter sparks and all that."

Winwick had, anyway, satisfied himself that he would certainly be amongst the first to write up the Draycott Apocalypse, and he composed and addressed a formal letter asking for permission to view the book. It was still, it seemed, in the ownership of the country family who had given their name to the work. He hoped he had offered the appropriate mingling of authority and deference in his application: the college arms upon the notepaper, and some mild flattery about the family's dedicated guardianship of so important a relic. And it seemed that he had: an invitation promptly followed. The Draycotts, of Draycott Hall, in the village, or rather hamlet, of Draycott (for there appeared to be no church), in some dim region of Northamptonshire, seemed to have dwindled to a single scion, named by Burns as Miss Lily Draycott. He had given her first name with a slight sneering hiss, as if he did not quite approve, perhaps because it had, in his day, been bestowed upon actresses and courtesans.

The place was, at least, only a fairly short journey from Winwick's college, but it was a dispiriting one, through wan fenland, and across low, dun, ridges faint against a dwindling winter sky. There was no-one to meet him at the station, but the directions supplied, in a hand of rather quavery dark ink, showed that he had a walk of about forty minutes ahead of him. There was a chill breeze to face, which bit at the delicate spirals of his ears, and whetted its teeth too on his rather austere nose. He strode on as resolutely as he could, and all around saw only frosted fields and hedgerows, coated with a clinging white fire.

The hall, when at length it glimmered into view in a sort of dreary haze across descending moorland, was of a pale, friable, weathered stone, and as he approached Winwick found himself thinking that it looked almost as if its very walls had been made of timeworn parchment: there was the same dry, dusty appearance. It stood far back from the nearest road, behind a screen of larch trees, whose thin limbs rattled in the bitter air.

Most of the windows, on the three rather squatting storeys that could be made out, still wore shutters, scarred by the winds and with paint peeling in grey flakes, as if they were the scales of some creature sloughing off old skin as it slept. The doorway was not a grand gesture, as so often in country houses, but a simple, low, almost square dark slot in the walls. Winwick looked about, but there appeared to be no bell, only a brass knocker rimed with a green crust, in a twisted shape that might have been intended once for an elephant's trunk. Perhaps, Winwick reflected, one of the Draycotts had been a servant of the empire and had installed this curio as a remembrance. He seized the brazen coil, which, despite the bleak wind, had a tingle of warmth to it, as if it had caught the rays of an unseen sun, and rapped it against the door.

The woman who answered his hollow knock after a short echoing silence wore a long dark gown relieved only by a scarlet, silken sash around her waist, from which depended a peal of silver and bronze keys. It was difficult to tell her age from her appearance: there were no obvious signs of wear in the amber-tinted skin of her long face, and her eyes still seemed to have a lively glimmer. But a great tower of silvery-black hair suggested the passage of a certain number of years, at least. She gestured to him to follow her along a stone passageway, and ushered him into a bare parlour where a table was carefully set out for a meal. He had not been certain at first whether he had been met by a housekeeper, or the chatelaine herself, and had proceeded with circumspection: but his doubts were resolved when she proffered her hand, elaborately festooned with gems, and he gave this the briefest of touches. She gestured him to a chair, and poured a dank wine into the glass before him. Then she signalled with a fluttering motion, almost like a blessing, over the silver chafing-dishes, and they served themselves. When the genteel scraping and clattering had subsided, his host addressed him once more.

"We are extra parochial, you understand."

He could certainly imagine that the obscurity of the place would make its inhabitants more than usually interested only in their own local affairs, but it seemed an odd beginning. Her black, glistening eyes, rather like skinned grapes, detected his confusion.

"I mean that we do not here belong to any parish—we are quite free from all civic or ecclesiastical interference. Usually that is only the case where the land formerly belonged to an abbey or to the throne. But here, neither ever applied. So it is not clear to historians why we have been left alone."

There was almost a melancholy fall to her last words, and her eyes glinted in the glow from the corroded candlesticks. Her long fingers, ornamented with the many bizarre rings, which were twisted like serpents around the waxen sticks of flesh, wafted once more in the dim light.

"In those days, Mr. Wanwick, it was said men feared the Church, the King, and the Devil, in that order. Since we have never had any very obvious affinity with the first two, it has sometimes been supposed that we must have thrown in our lot with the, ah, *junior* partner—d'you see?"

She laughed to herself, in a series of throaty surges that were not unlike a purring.

Her visitor smiled weakly.

"Actually, it's Winwick," he murmured. But his hostess appeared not to hear him.

"Be that as it may, if we can hardly say that we have ever *flourished* as a family, yet we have at least enjoyed a long decay."

Winwick felt these phrases had been deployed before.

"Charming place . . . warm welcome," he muttered. His feeble remarks went unregarded.

"You know the meddler, Mr. Wanwick?" he heard her ask.

Her guest cast about anxiously in his mind for any of his acquaintances who might be regarded as unusually meddlesome. Perhaps Burns was meant, who had put him in touch?

"Well, I . . . "

"The medlar fruit. It may only be taken when it is in decay. And then, I say, a very noble taste: autumn leaves and sweet dates. We nurture it here. In the old orchard."

There was a slight emphasis on the word *old*, as if to imply that there had been many other fruit groves since this original.

Winwick expressed polite interest, but this was lost in the next remark.

"As with that rare fruit, so with some old families, perhaps. Finest in decay."

It was difficult to know how to respond with politeness to this, without admitting either that he discerned the decay or that he disputed the fineness, so Hugo Winwick allowed a silence to elapse, before attempting the brief speech of thanks he had mentally composed and refined on his train journey and on the brisk walk from the station.

" . . . particularly as I understand you have already given your most generous hospitality to scholars before me . . . "

Miss Draycott had been regarding him with the sort of amused and inquisitive look one might bestow upon a pet that has learnt a new and slightly unexpected trick, until he petered out with this final remark.

She sighed, disturbing the candles, whose amber flames flickered as if shrinking back in dismay.

"Perhaps you would like to go to the *Revelation* now, Mr. Wanwick?"

Miss Draycott rose, with a rustle of her dress, which had the dark polish of old mahogany. The pleats seemed to shimmer in the candle-light like black flames.

⁊◌

The manuscript was kept in a casket in an upper room, which had a single arched window. It was barely furnished with a riddled wooden table and a chair whose legs ended in worn claws. And it was cold: the bleak wind that had assailed him on his walk to the hall was not kept out here, but seemed to whisper and moan in the crevices of the walls. He rubbed his fingers together, and carefully raised the great dark binding of the book before him.

As Burns had surmised, the book was indeed bound up with other, wholly secular material. So far as Winwick could make out, on a rapid examination, there was, firstly, some sort of treatise on orchardry, full of the shapes of trees that he certainly did not recognise: some bearing fruit that appeared to possess the ability to grimace and stare. There was an herball, among whose illustrations he noticed a mandrake, a moly, and a monkshood, together with blooms stranger still, possessed of limbs like twisted homunculi. After that came a set of pages indited with archaic symbols, angular and, as it were, stalking over the page. There was perhaps a hint of Hebrew in their calligraphy too, or some even older language, which he did not have the time to examine more thoroughly. And then, at last, as he turned the pages ever more eagerly, there came the apocalypse itself, and Winwick dwelled upon each leaf with wonder. This was one of the most strongly imagined he had ever seen.

The figures had been drawn in fine black ink first, and the colour added by means of a tinted wash. This was, he knew, a special craft secret of English illuminators, more subtle than the smears of raw pigment used elsewhere. It was particularly suitable, Winwick noticed, to depict the proper colour of an English sea: the grey-green was admirably achieved, and much more realistic than the bright blaring blue of convention, which might just about do for the Mediterranean. It was a delicate, careful art, which seemed apt for the limners at work in a rain-washed and misty island. He turned the pages with a quick delight, the zeal of the scholar leaping up inside him, and the desire to be the first chronicler of this exquisite masterpiece crackling within him.

The realism had also been applied, he thought, to the rather splendid seven-headed, crowned and horned serpent or dragon. It looked like something that just might have been drawn out from the dreary depths of some English fen to confront and carry off all the kingdom's sinners. Despite its beady eyes and lashing red tongues, its slime-coloured scales and spurred wings, there was just the faintest air of melancholy to it. He looked at the human figure painted as if writhing before the monster. Perhaps, he thought, rather too irreverently, the beast was disappointed because its prey did not have a face that it could threaten.

For here was one part where the Draycott Apocalypse, which otherwise seemed remarkably intact, was indeed incomplete. There were no features on the believer confronted by the dragon with seven heads: everything else was limned in, their body, limbs, clothes, shoes, and they were even depicted under a withered black fig tree, but they had no face. For some reason the artist had simply stopped short.

Winwick looked at the pale oval carefully, bringing his gaze close to it, in case he could detect any signs of erasure. There were very slight, minute ripples in the paper, which for a moment gave the impression of quivering. He narrowed his eyes and stared even more intently. Was there the merest hint of a skein of flesh coloured in there, or was that the fading of the manuscript? But, yes, the pink tint began to seem more substantial, and he even felt he could discern the smudges of eyes, ears, and nose. He drew back, to look away and give his eyes a rest, blinking. And then he regarded the picture once more. The seven-headed monster in its hues of English mud and rain and marsh still glimmered upon the page, and its victim's clothes had their autumn hues of scarlet and gold and brown. But the white void, the solemn blank mask, on top of the figure's shoulders, indeed seemed much more defined now. It was certainly possible to make out the lineaments of some of the features. The eyes were a wan grey, the ears rather like delicate shells, and the nose, narrow and sensitive. As if in a paper mirror, Hugo Winwick found himself staring at his own face.

Something that might have been the wind roared among the walls of the room.

The Seer of Trieste

Trieste, tristesse, they say, city of sweet sadness, the ghostly cousin of Venice across the gulf, clinging to its Italian verge below the vast and Slavic karst, the lost imperial sea-port, abandoned gatehouse to the lands of the East, forever swept by the bitter wind of the *Bora*, which makes its wailings in all the old, decaying streets and squares. But that does not do justice to its other character, to its air of insouciance, to its wry independence, and its persistent allegiance to the outlandish in the arts and literature—and magic.

I came here with a stipend from a certain trust to research the work of Captain Sir Richard Francis Burton, soldier, explorer, linguist, sexologist, first or fullest translator of the *Arabian Nights* and the *Kama Sutra*, and for a while the British Vice-Consul to Trieste. A sinecure, they told him in London, anxious to be rid of him and to thrust him as far away as possible. Plenty of time to do what you please. He disliked the brisk and mercantile outlet of the Austria-Hungarian double-eagled Empire that Trieste then was, and lived when he could in a tavern at some remove: but even his quite nominal duties meant he could not evade its streets forever. And it was thus, I believe, that he first encountered the spirit of Trieste, and wrestled with it in his work, to be followed in this by certain other exiles and outcasts.

When I say spirit, I do not mean some nebulous pervading "tone". No: I refer to the great form that I learnt is its secret

81

symbol and in some sense its guardian. The city's emblem is a golden fleur-de-lys on a scarlet ground. That will do quite well for civic and ceremonial purposes: neat, heraldic, hinting at a proud medieval past it doesn't in fact have. But it is not the real crest of Trieste, its living sigil. That is far different. How I found out what that was, and what it had done with Burton and—I see I can no longer avoid invoking his name too—Giacomo Joyce, well that is what I shall now recount.

I suppose it is well-known that Isobel, Lady Burton, burnt many of the papers of her husband upon his death, for she did not like what she read, an act of literary vandalism that moved even the gentle poet Ernest Dowson to pen a poem of reproof against her. Yet what exactly was destroyed, and what survived, had never been definitely established. It was my task to catalogue the work consigned to the flames, as far as it might be retrieved from descriptions in Burton's letters and other texts: a sort of ghostly catalogue of perished books. But I was also to look out for fragments of his writings that had eluded his righteous spouse, and that was why I was in Trieste, for it was here if anywhere that they might be run to earth.

The trust had found for me an apartment on the uppermost floor of via Roma 23, a broad stone building in umber peppered with the black of traffic fumes, for the street is a busy thoroughfare. I entered through a deep rounded arch and porch, like the approach to some dark chasm up in the mountains on which Trieste turns its disdainful back. Two doors with glinting brass handles and opaque tinted glass gave onto a gloomy, bare hallway, and there was a flight of elegant stairs, with scrolled iron balustrades, up to my rooms, entered by a door of varnished oak. Opposite mine was another, for the only other occupant of the floor, and to one side of this a small strip of fading paper in a silver niche read: "M. Peterlin/Istituto Astrosofico".

I was made curious by this, of course, but my work kept me preoccupied for my first few weeks in the city. As well as collating all the references I could to works by Burton that had never in fact appeared, I also went into the back streets of the city, up its cobbled slopes and between its narrow buildings, becoming used to their prevalent colours of old ochre and soft brown, seeking out the bookshops and junkshops that might harbour some forgotten fragment of his prose or verse. I did not find any. But thus busied, I saw no glimpse of my neighbour until one evening, in the lemony dusk that comes upon the old town, I had looked up from my desk in pause and was gazing out of my window to the broad street below. I observed a tall, lean, silver-haired man, with a long dark coat and narrow-brimmed hat, hurry across the road and enter our building. His footsteps made their mark upon the echoing stairs. That, then, must be Mr. Peterlin. I was wearied after a day's close note-taking, and wanted a change. I thought I might introduce myself.

He greeted me at the door, politely, but said: "It is too late for a consultation." I tried to explain myself in my crude Italian and, detecting my accent, he at once switched to English, and invited me inside. I entered what can only be dignified by the word "*camerata*": our terse "room" would not do it justice. It was sumptuously furnished, with beautifully brocaded peacock-blue-and-gold wallpaper, woven rugs and carpets in intricate patterns, and stately, silk-backed chairs.

My host looked at me, amused. "You are surprised, I see. Suffice only to say my family was once of great account here: we held office under the King and Emperor. This is what is left of that. For myself, I do what I can. And that is how I speak your tongue. See . . . "

He showed me a card offering his services as a cultural guide to the city, and quickly listed its luminaries: Charles Lever, Richard Burton, James Joyce, Thomas Mann, Sigmund

Freud, Italo Svevo, the bookseller and poet Umberto Saba, its fine symbolist artist Cesare Sofianopulo, its *designatrice*, the modernist architect Teodora. "I can tell you about all of these," he said.

"I publish also," he added, and proffered first a pocket-book with a folding map, the *Piccola Guida per Tutti*. Then, more hesitantly, a sort of almanac in beige paper wrappers, the *Calendro Familiare L'Astrologo*, with saints' days, notable anniversaries and so on all shown, with advertisements for patisseries, wireless shops, funeral stationers, palmists and florists, and with, as I found by politely flicking through, an astrological chapter with a segmented and symbol-strewn circle. "I have a talent for that sort of thing," he said, dismissively, "and you: what brings you to Trieste?"

He knew all about Captain Burton, of course. He could recite all the main facts of his life and the places in the city that he had grudgingly visited, and did so almost tonelessly, as he might for a client. But when I mentioned my quest for unpublished writings, his eyes—unTriestine eyes, a very pale blue—caught mine more intently. We quickly began to talk together as if we had known each other very long, familiarly, as strangers sometimes will. At length, in a lull in our conversation—

"Do you know some men called him a monster?" he said. "That is very strange to me. A monster, because he dared confront the very things that are surely our essence: the sex urge and the death urge. Yet, because of what I know, I laugh at it too."

"What is it you know?" I replied.

He smiled, a slight and wistful gesture.

"Not yet, my new friend. Not yet the secrets of Trieste. But you shall know, I promise you. In the meantime, let me put it to you in this way. Captain Burton has produced some interesting minor works before he comes to Trieste, but they are not his really great work: that is to come, his *Kama Sutra*, his *Arabian Nights*. Mr. James Joyce, he too has done some poems and stories, but nothing so ground-breaking as what he will start here. Also, there is a third here now—the same thing there, with him. What does that tell you?"

"That they came to Trieste at the peak of their careers and found sufficient repose to work hard at what they wanted."

"No. That they were guided by the spirit of Trieste."

"Oh, if you like," I said, in a mollifying mood. "Yes, the city was good for them."

"That is certainly not what I like. What I like is this: I am a scholar of the stars, that you know. I see also the major principles that prevail in a place, the *djinn* if you like Burton's term. Trieste has such. Like the works that these men produced, it is a monstrous thing. And that is because it is there in all they did. Now,"—this, with decision, as if taking the conversation in a different direction—"you would like very much to find some unknown Burton, yes? I shall see what can be done."

I was startled and excited at the same time. "You know where it might be found?"

"Where it exists, yes."

"Where—?"

"In the mind of what I have called the major principle, which is also the monster."

"Ah." I must have looked, and sounded, more than suspicious. Spirit writings I knew all too much about. When I was researching the "Golden Road to Samarkand" poet, James Elroy Flecker, I had been offered some new verses by his disembodied soul, channelled by a Mr. Wallis Mansford. However, as he also claimed to be in contact with Shelley, Keats, Wilde, Robert Burns, and Omar Khayyam, and was apparently undaunted either by Broad Scots or Classical Persian, I felt justified in having some reservations about this work.

"Tsch, tsch, you are so very literal. Paper, paper, that is all you want. Do you think such a great man left his impress here only upon paper? But if that is so important, you should go and see the other Englishman. He will, I am sure, become the third great countryman of yours to make his master-work here. And he has a letter to Burton."

I let pass that Joyce, an Irishman, was not quite the compatriot he thought.

"A letter *to* Burton? Who is he?"

And Mr. Peterlin told me.

ဢ

It was by no means easy to find the studio of Stephen Thessaly, for it was sequestered away on the upper slopes of the city, close to the steep steps leading, through labyrinthine walled alleys, to the botanical garden. About three quarters of a way up these a riddled grey-wooded door was set into a blind wall. I pushed at it, and it gave in with a jar. There, belying the forbidding entrance, was a modest single-floor shack—it could only be called that—with a sloping roof, in a court-yard of lichen and creepers and dead leaves, which virtually covered it. I heard a murmuring from within. Cautiously, I looked through a grimy window, thrusting aside the rampant vegetation. I could make out a squat form resident on a pile of rugs, but the room was as if enveloped in a murky green veil, caused I thought not solely by the streaked ichors upon the pane. The figure's head moved undulatingly from side to side and its arms at intervals seemed to do likewise. The murmuring rose and fell like an incantation. I waited until there had been an appreciable silence, and then entered as softly as I could. Green fumes rose from a thurible dangling from the ceiling, giving a miasmic taint to the thick air of the shack. The idol-like form barely moved at first. Then its eyes blinked open and regarded me with a watery gaze. A serpentine, rather grey-fleshed arm gestured to me to sit. Finding nothing else, I crouched upon the floor, and stated my business. Thessaly reached into a coffer of sandalwood, where a yellowing curl resided upon a sarsenet of blue. He produced it with another flourish of his dingy flesh.

"Oh, yes. I have it here. It is from Forster Fitzgerald Arbuthnot, who collaborated with him on the *Kama Sutra*. They had something much bigger in mind after that. Oh yes, much bigger." And he sniggered at a private joke.

It was on crumpled paper in a sloping, looping hand. I took it from him eagerly. It read, after unimportant preliminaries: "Send me the first limb of Shiva, the <u>Lingam</u>." The last word was underlined. It was impossible to tell whether this was for emphasis, or to denote a title. And if a title, did that reference to the *first* limb mean, as would be certainly so, that the lingam was prime in importance in Shiva: or that there were more limbs to follow? It was all very tantalising.

"You are wondering," he pronounced, "what old FFA meant." The familiar way of referring to Burton's friend also caused him amusement, and he repeated it; "Old FFA . . . " Well, I *was* wondering, and said so.

And it emerged that Thessaly was quite certain he knew. "Through a certain process," he said, "which Mr. Peterlin is perfecting, I have had insight into what Burton and Arbuthnot"—he made them sound incongruously like a firm of respectable solicitors—"were up to. The *Kama Sutra* was *as nothing* to this," he went on, "no wonder Lady Burton *quailed*, poor dear. Tantric, you know. Tantric. Very much so. Of course, you understand the *Lingam*, which I am convinced she saw, was just the first. There must have been seven more. But *one* was quite enough for her, I'm sure."

I made a rapid mental inventory of the images of Shiva. They varied, of course. But usually I made it four arms, two legs, one lingam. Seven.

"Eight?" I asked.

"Eight," Thessaly replied, firmly. "There must have been eight."

"The eighth was?"

He was unflustered, became sly. "Ah, wouldn't we all like to know. That must be the very secret of them all. Perhaps it was Shiva's third eye. But, if so, what did it 'see', if we must use that term? Well," he became confiding, "I am sure I shall very soon find out. For all that I am so very thrilled by what Burton was doing, and of course by that *gargantuan* and *grotesque* work of Joyce's, they were, you understand, merely preparing the way for me. I am to be the culmination.

"But how, you will naturally ask, go beyond them? By going beyond language, of course. A mere book will no longer do. We now need an art that is a fully physical experience, one which embraces all the eight senses, comprising scent, sound, touch, taste, sight, kinesis, the sex sense, and of course the psychic sense. You perhaps happened upon some of my experimentations when you arrived? Well, you are the first to do so. You shall be able to proudly boast that you knew in its first stages Stephen Thessaly's *Octet*. A simple title for so great a thing, isn't it? But of course it could hardly be called anything else."

℘

I returned to the via Roma and entered again through the gaping cave. As I ascended the stairs, I thought the silence of the place was somehow more tangible than usual, that the leaved doors had shut out more than the sound of the busy street. I paused outside my neighbour's apartment, appreciating again the silver sign, with his name and singular profession. Then I knew that I must go in. A prickling of the flesh swept over me, both stimulating and disturbing, as if it were a movement in Mr. Thessaly's sensual composition. I pushed gently at the door.

I saw through the dimness of his room a great oak lectern and upon this lay an open book of black leather whose burnished clasps fell in gleaming shards of silver on either side. There was nothing on its tall pale leaves. On either side two slender candles glowed, and within their penumbra stood two boys, all dressed in white tunics of a Renaissance style, which had the look of silk and cambric, and complete with a tilted white beret and aigrette: and they were gazing solemnly upon the volume. At first I thought they must be part of some rite my neighbour was preparing for the grand *Maschere*, the Masked Ball, the one night of riot the old prim trading city permits, which was to be held that evening. That, however, it soon became clear, was just a convenient pretext for procuring the costumes, for dressing the boys as he had.

The subtle light of old amber played around their countenances, and there was something in the scene of an incaught expectancy, a hesitation in the order of things. I stared, as they stared, at the bare skeins of the book. One of the boys, frowning in concentration, exhaled quickly and the candles flickered under his breath. They caused a gavotte of shadows to play upon the book as if they were trying to conjure up characters there. Both of the boys looked startled, and trepidation leapt into their dark eyes.

Peterlin rose from his high carved chair, scarlet-cushioned and studded with brass grotesques, and his brittle blue eyes from out of the lean patrician face caught mine. He placed a finger upon his lips, and then whispered to the two boys, who went into an adjoining room. When they emerged, they had changed into the clothes of any street urchin, with open-necked shirts and shin-length shorts and soft shoes. Coins dropped into their proffered brown palms, and they scampered off.

I stared at my neighbour. Peterlin peered back at me, as if nothing untoward had happened. Then he relented.

"There was an old trick of Ficino's Renaissance science, or magic. You have just witnessed my attempt to revive it. Take two virgin boys, a blank parchment, and candle-light. Meditate upon what passages in the celestial books you wish to read. They will appear, written in scarlet majuscules. You must use white pages, both for the boys and the books. Of course, he does say you should scourge the boys first, so that the crimson ink from their bodies calls down that from above, but I did not think I could go that far, even with disowned waifs. Perhaps that was the flaw. Next time . . . " his voice faded away, his wistful smile played upon his lips, then he recovered himself.

"Come, my friend, we are due at the *Maschere*. All I will say to you is this: watch very carefully all the players, all the guises, and report back to me later what you see." He would say no more.

I did as he asked. It was no burden to do so, for the great gilded chamber of the Tripcovich Hall was one teeming mass of colourfully costumed masquers: green-faced clowns, monks with fauns' ears, horned devils, harlequins, skull-faced harlots in scarlet dresses, ballerinas in black veils, tail-coated women, Renaissance princes, pale pierrots, a sphinx, an heraldic lion, several angels. It was a gorgeous and panting, pulsing scene, and I thought how old Burton would have relished it. That thought was not mine alone: for someone had dressed as him, with wild hair and whiskers, frock coat and an ornamental sword, and had caught his hard-eyed look very well too. They must have studied his portraits.

Was he the character that Peterlin wanted me to see? Nothing remarkable there, surely. But then, floating above all the heads of the revellers I caught glimpses of a mottled, a blotchy dun and olive coloured mask, spheroid, with dank slits for eyes. I could not see what costume followed below, because I only saw the visage from a distance, hovering slightly above the throng, and undulating in a most peculiar motion, like something swimming very tentatively in an unknown sea. The whirl of the ball whisked me on, and I lost sight of it, but again later it came to the corner of my eye, a dull but dappled blur of a head, with mere shifts of shadow where the eyes must look out. And then it seemed as if it held all of the writhing figures below it within its influence, as if it was making them dance.

I thought of the many meetings and partings, the fleeting recognitions and attractions, the stories unmeshed and untold, the infinite variations possible between all these dancers and all the disguises they had adopted. All the things that would not be, when they dissolved back into the dust of day. And it suddenly seemed it could not be so. It came to me that there must be, somewhere, a multitudinous forking of moments, a stream of infinite rearrangements of the one route we knew here below.

∞

In the brittle blue light of morning, with the red fleur-de-lys flags in the Piazza de la Unita flopped upon their poles, there were discarded black felt and paper masks in the gutters and niches of the streets, and even peculiar props left lying around: a trident, a tin bugle, a tube of green lipstick, a unicorn's silver horn, a set of whiskers stuck to a stone globe. I stood on the end of the stone tongue that sticks out into the Adriatic, the jetty, the justly-called Molo Audace, and drank in the sea's topaz iridescence. Below me, in the clear, lapping water, curious yellow weeds waved. My friend from via Roma 23 joined me and we stood contemplatively together. At length: "Well," he said, "you shall see."

Mr. Peterlin led me up the broad but dingy stairs of the city's Natural History Museum, had a word with the attendant, and led me through its rooms with their white horse skeleton, preserved and pinioned butterflies, stuffed wild cats and weasels with faded fur, ammonites, ancient vertebrae, and the wings and antennae of what weird, primeval things caught in amber I could not say. At the door of one room, from which a mephitic stench emanated, he paused, then ushered me respectfully in.

There was one cabinet only, in the centre of the room, a great glass case visible from all sides and illuminated from below like a huge lantern, in a sickly light. Inside this was a jar, a cylinder of thick, pale greenish glass: and this held a fluid of a most vile colour. Within that, there hung a vast, preserved octopus. Its brooding presence filled not only its bottle prison but the whole empty room. I stared at it in appalled fascination. It was an ugly and unorientating enough exhibit. But that was not all. For this was the mask—or this was the face—that I had seen lunging above the cavorting crowds at the *Maschere*.

"There is a live one in the aquarium, by the *Molo*, too," observed Peterlin, rather inconsequentially.

We walked back to our rooms in the via Roma, silently. But Peterlin had not done with me yet.

In the subdued light of his room he eyed me curiously, as if gauging the effect of his revelation.

"Have you ever noticed," he said, "how often the colours grey-green, yellow-green, brown-green, and indeed snot-green and gamboge, recur in *Ulysses*? Go back and look. So very often. There is a reason for that. They were what was before the author as he wrote his notes and his vast novel, they were the hues of the true beast of Trieste, whose tentacled spirit he had invoked to aid him, as Burton had before him. Why do you think his alternative title for his book was, as his letters show, *Upon a Grey Sea*? For that was how all things seemed to him as he wrote on, under the command of that old, old ocean denizen: they seemed one great grey solid sea.

"It is certainly true," I said, "that some might think *Ulysses* reads as though it were written by an intelligent octopus that was grappling for the first time with English."

Peterlin shook his head. "You are mocking me. It was written by Joyce, of course. And mostly, it must be said, in that sheep of a city, Zürich. But it was here that he formed the idea for it, here that it began, and here he wrote the important chapters, for he was possessed by the spirit of Trieste: that much his many letters and notes show; and it went with him. You now know what that spirit is.

"Besides," he continued, "you are missing something really obvious. The world has the one huge work that Joyce delivered up to it, for sure. But do you think that is all there is? Certainly not. While his hand wrote what the creature inspirited in him, there were of course attached to him seven other unseen hands, all devising their other, separate, sprawling stories; these are the seven lost books of *Ulysses*. They are still here, in the psychic space of the city, in the air of Trieste, in its spirit chapters, waiting to descend upon any willing and well-prepared pages. That is what Ficino's Florentine sorcery will help me find. You will see."

For a moment, sitting there in the rooms of the via Roma 23, it all seemed horribly plausible. But what had I seen? A preserved octopus in a tank. Someone at the masked ball who had had the bright idea of emulating it. They were elusive, true, and curiously elevated above the crowd, but that might not mean much. A few stray references in *Ulysses*, as Peterlin averred: but anything might be found in that cabbala of a book. And a fragment of a hint, no more, about the Victorian Vice-Consul's final work of erotica.

So I nodded my head slowly, rose, and we shook hands, he looking at me keenly. I wished him well in his experiments.

Soon after, my work complete, I was obliged to leave Trieste and return to England. The world still awaits Stephen Thessaly's great multi-sensual masterwork, *Octet*, the revelation of the seven lost books of *Ulysses* and, for that matter, the great *Eight Limbs of Shiva*, the relentless sexual epic, the Tantric bible, upon which Captain Burton and his distant amanuensis, Forster Fitzgerald Arbuthnot, were apparently engaged. And yet still, I am sure, my friend Mr. Peterlin, the seer of Trieste, at via Roma 23, is striving to help make them exist.

Three Strange Places

The Axholme Toll

I t was Stevenson, I think, who most notably observed that there are some places that simply demand a story should be told of them. Such was the case with the Isle of Erraid, a tidal islet off Mull, where he stayed as a young man while assisting his father with his profession as a lighthouse engineer. It led to his story "The Merry Men", full of the wild lore of the sea. There are many such tales told of islands, which seem always to draw the imagination of the mainlander, and to nourish their own myths too. Yet I wonder if there are not also enclaves within the solid land of the country, which are islands in a different sense. They are somehow set apart from the rest of the everyday world. We enter them, and a sense steals over us of being in a different domain. Some subtle change in the terrain tells us that we are not quite wholly in a reliable realm. For me, the Isle of Axholme, in the far north-western marge of Lincolnshire, will always figure as exactly such a place, for it was indeed once an island, and it is still remote and peculiar.

It was, as I say, until the seventeenth century, a real inland island, surrounded by three rivers at their widest span, traversable only by ferry. Even within the bounds these formed, much of the terrain was inhospitable marshland, whose narrow tracks only natives knew thoroughly. It was the practice for the isle folk to stalk these murky wastes on nimble stilts, and there was competition to be deftest at this unusual skill. Drainage by Dutch engineers under charter from Charles I ended its isolation a little, but it retained a distinctive character for quite a while afterwards. Islonians, as they call themselves, are proud of their particular family names and still refer to "the Isle", even though it is strictly not that any longer. In fact, it was always a series of islands: one long ridge in the middle, bearing four villages upon it, some outlying outcrops, and a cluster of ferry settlements by the river banks.

I found that its mysteries began in the Dark Ages, when some astral catastrophe or other—a fireball, or so it is inferred—spread flame even through its wateriness, burning trees down to their roots deep underground, and denuding it for a while of vegetation. Modern conspiracists regard this as one sign among many of the cogency of the prophecies of Ezekiel. It has also been claimed as the true locality of Avalon—the fact of it being an island only accessible with difficulty, and the deceptive similarity of its name, being in its favour. Against that, however, is the sad absence of any other Arthurian links, or of orchards, for Avalon is generally held to mean "Isle of Apples".

It has also had, through the ages, other reputations. Not surprisingly, its remoteness bred talk of magic, and it is said to have had a hermit-wizard in occupation for a century or so, on one of its lonelier knolls. The Templars, too, are naturally said to have had a priory here: although, in fact, it seems to have been Carthusian. There are astrological links, suggesting a lost zodiac, known now only by an old local saying, "'Tis Scorpio in Crowle" (the latter being the northernmost village on its spine), meaning a time of ill omen.

Then, it has its own literary mystery too. In April 1903, the publisher John Lane received a parcel through the post at his London offices in Vigo Street, under the sign of The Bodley Head. It contained the manuscript of a novel. There was nothing uncommon about that, of course: except that the manuscript had no sign of the author, and no title, and there was no accompanying letter. Nor was there any indication where it had come from. It arrived in a red box, and that was just about all that could be known about it.

The work was sent to the publisher's reader in the usual way, and he reported favourably. As was his habit with anything out of the ordinary, John Lane then read it himself. He had made his name in the Eighteen Nineties as the publisher of "daring" and "modern" books that came to epitomise the period as the "Naughty Nineties", especially in his Keynotes series of novels. He also issued his flagship periodical *The Yellow Book*, which gave its name to the decade: the Yellow Nineties. It was, at first anyway, embellished with some of the audacious black-and-white drawings of Aubrey Beardsley. Their boldness, and the bright gold covers, soon made sure it was seen and hotly discussed.

But by 1903, John Lane had mellowed more into the role of a mainstream publisher. He was a shrewd businessman, who liked to be on good terms with his authors and to social-ise with them: but still had a keen-eyed understanding of the exact commercial value of their work. The previous year, he had scored a success with Kenneth Grahame's gentle pastoral pieces, *Dream Days*, with a verse play, *Ulysses* by Stephen Phillips (compared in his day to Shakespeare, Milton and Tennyson), and (rather more in the vein of the book before him), a rip-roaring historical study, *King Monmouth* by Allan Fea. Still, a strong seller in fiction had really eluded him. He was ready to find one.

When he looked at the untitled book, he agreed with his reader's assessment. The mystery manuscript was a great historical romance in the tradition of Stevenson and Scott, about the seventeenth century struggle between the proud and independent people of the Isle of Axholme in Lincolnshire and the Dutch drainage lords who had come to change their world forever, and drive them from their lands. It was a gripping, twisting and turning, swashbuckling, yet also thoughtful and sometimes eerie book, with the isolated marshlands of Axholme so strongly evoked that the reader almost felt they had lived there themselves.

Accordingly, Lane decided to publish the book. But how to do so, without even a title, and no author? No doubt with an eye to the publicity value, he placed an advertisement in the press:

To AUTHORS. NOTICE.—If the Writer of an Historical Novel without Title, Author's Name, or Address, sent some weeks ago to The Bodley Head in a Red Box, will communicate with the Publisher, he will hear something to his advantage.

– John Lane, Vigo Street, London, W.2.

"Hear something to his advantage"! It was the very phrase used by solicitors in mystery novels when a large or unusual legacy awaits the hero. The notice had the desired effect. It created what one newspaper called a "hullabaloo of excitement". Yet no author came forward. The publisher tried again, with a further notice, saying he would publish the book at a certain date unless he heard from the author. This, of course, was very cleverly stoking up the interest in the book, and some acid commentators thought it was all just a stunt. But it was not.

John Lane went ahead and published the book as *The MS. in a Red Box*, and it has been known by this title ever since. After all the discussion leading up to its appearance, it was not surprising that it sold well. So much might be expected. But, gratifyingly for Lane's and his reader's judgement, critics and the public agreed about its qualities. It had an enthralling, well-devised plot, the right blend of adventure and love interest, the historical setting was just familiar enough but also original and unusual; and the island scenes were strange and appealing to the reader. Indeed, the Axholme dimension may have had much to do with the book's success: it was seen as a curious and inaccessible region still.

After the book came out, it is said Lane received many letters claiming authorship, but none of them were at all convincing. Two things, however, were tolerably clear about the author. He was a proficient, very capable prose writer and storyteller: and he knew the Isle of Axholme and its people and history intimately well.

Much of the book is a vivid, pretty brisk adventure story: the tale of Frank Vavasour, son of a local squire, who leads the revolt against the Dutch clearances, aided by loyal friends, betrayed by squinting villiains, and never near enough to the arms of the vivacious woman he loves, who is inconveniently the daughter of a Dutch doctor—though a fair-minded and moderate man. But there is also a strangeness about the book, caused by its Axholme setting: there are weird visions and curses, and the sense of an inexorable working-out of fate. In one episode, young Vavasour, hotly pursued by the King's men, takes to the green alleys of the marshes, where their horses cannot go because of the treacherous terrain. And yet, it still seems to him that he is pursued, for over the wastes there comes to him the drumming of hooves where no horses could possibly be; and he wonders what riders these beasts must bear. No more is said of the matter; Vavasour evades his predators, but the reader is left to think that the phantom author is hinting here at more than he can tell.

A strong candidate for the authorship has been put forward in recent years, to the extent that some editions now definitely attribute it to him, and so does the catalogue of the British Library. This is the Reverend John Arthur Hamilton

(1854-1924), who was a minister of the Congregational Church at Crowle, in Axholme, from 1870 to 1878: only eight years, but perhaps important ones, for he was very young and it was his first pastorate. He later went on to hold office at Saltaire, Yorkshire from 1878 to 1896, and finally in Penzance from 1897 until his death. He gave his house in Cornwall the name "Axholme". This suggests the Isle remained steadfast in his memory.

This John Hamilton was an author. He pioneered the idea of sermons written as stories for children. His books include *A Mountain Path and Forty Three Other Talks for Young Children* (Low & Co, 1894), *The Life of John Milton, Partly In His Own Words* (Congregational Union, 1908), *The Giant and the Caterpillar and Other Addresses to Young People* (Allenson, 1912), and *The Wonderful River and Other Addresses to Young People* (Allenson, 1913). Somewhat more to the point, he also wrote at least one historical romance—*Captain John Lister: a Tale of Axholme* (Hutchinson, 1906)—set in the time of the English Civil War. But to that he put his name.

Yet all—bar one—of these worthy titles are not in the least like *The MS. in a Red Box*. That book is full-blooded, vigorous, and very rarely pious. This could, of course, be the reason why the author wanted it only issued anonymously. But could a man who had already put his name to these other books resist claiming authorship in some way for a work that must have cost him many hours of work, hours diverted from his more sacred duties? And could a cleric who was so concerned to mix story-telling with an improving message completely resist the opportunity to do so in this work too? Certainly, he could have sent the book to Lane anonymously, in the red box, just as Lane recounted: or collaborated with him on an elaborate hoax.

It was in the hope of throwing more light upon this literary mystery that I made my way to the Isle one day in late summer. I may as well confess now that I learnt very little new as to the book, or its author: but what I encountered instead gave me ample cause to remember the Isle well.

Axholme does not attract many visitors. There is a lot of ugliness within or in sight of it. Pylons, power stations, motorways, dredging operations, and the more obscure industrial plant are all too blatant upon it, and only escaped in its most hidden parts. Rashes of new houses make no attempt to emulate the local style—which at its quirkiest has hints of the Dutch influence—instead, they are often big, porticoed, and made of a pale brick, all starved of colour, as if no-one cared who built what here. I even saw one with gateposts topped by lions whose heads were painted bronze and bodies gold. Yet its real architectural riches are not to be seen: all but one church was padlocked, perhaps due to vandalism.

Still, there were hints of the Isle's inner richness, of what it might have been. The road from the most remote village, Wroot, following dead straight dikes for four or five miles north to Sandtoft, is little-used, since there is a major road to the east following a similar alignment. But as I drove, I passed fields where there hovered drifts of blue flax, ethereal as clear, still, sky-filled pools. And these were bordered on the roadside edge by blazons of bright red poppies and the white mist of daisies, so the experience was at moments like riding through a phantasmagoric parade. It was as if, I thought then, the Isle was trying to put forth at least one show of beauty in defiance of all that was around.

The Isle supports a weekly newspaper—actually about eight pages of local news wrapped around standardised media features from its parent press. It must be one of the few papers to bear a quotation from Tennyson upon its masthead: "Ring out the old, Ring in the new, Ring out the false, Ring in the true". The *Epworth Bells (& Crowle Advertiser)* has been published for 130 years. Among its fascinating pages, with the usual reports on fêtes, council meetings, juvenile delinquency, court appearances, there is a notice of High Water times on the Trent, which forms the Isle's eastern boundary. To this column is added the cryptic comment, seemingly straight out of some ancient almanac, "The Aegir usually appears during high spring and midwinter tides and arrives about two hours before high waters in Gainsborough, about three hours before in Owston Ferry . . . " Who or what, I naturally wondered, is the Aegir whose coming is so watched for? Some wrathful river-guardian?

Well, almost. It is a visible, lunging tidal current, rather like the Severn Bore, which broils the slow, broad waters of the Trent into foaming energy as it passes. The name, with its legendary ring, is of unknown origin. It would seem people do still gather to watch it pass, and talk about it as if it were a living thing: "Aegir's on its way" or "Aegir's strong today".

I was left with the clear impression that, despite the intrusion of industry, the diminishing of its island status by drainage and dual carriageways, and the rash of incomers commuting to Scunthorpe or Doncaster, it still does have a deep-buried differentness about it. And I felt there was some thread linking all the legends together, which had somehow been lost, but which might be rediscerned. If it was not Avalon, was it the last refuge of some other legendary figure? If the Templars were not here, was there some other order of knights or priests? If the place was somehow blasted, always to be barren and with ugliness thrust upon it, was there some reason for this? And was it only the Aegir that was watched for here?

Well, I had my answer to all those questions.

That winter I went back to Axholme, and took a cottage there at Christmas. I dislike that time of year, for I am by nature solitary and prefer nothing better than quietness and my own company, with a good fire and a good book. So it is a habit of mine to go away then, somewhere quite remote and unexpected, where I shall not be disturbed and the rites of the season can pass me by, unobserved. I confess, too, that the Isle had taken a hold of me, for all its hardness and harshness, and I wanted to reflect more upon its mysteries.

The place I took I had found in a notice in the *Epworth Bells*. It was an old ferry cottage, a simple, tall, redbrick building, with few rooms, which stood by a narrow track, which had once led down to the crossing; since that had closed many years ago, there was now little use for the track at all, and people seldom took it. Grass and moss grew down its middle and the hedges either side were thick and high. When I walked down the lane from the little station, bearing my modest luggage, there was still the skeleton of a hard white frost lingering from the morning, crusting the dark wood of the hedge and the rank green of the road with a lichen of white.

The house still belonged, through some long process of bureaucratic accretion, to a semi-somnolent drainage board, and they largely left it to itself, getting what meagre income they could from rentals. And since Axholme is hardly a prime place for visitors, it was often empty. A caretaker, from off-isle (as they say there) had charge of it, and apologised when I spoke to him that it would be rather cold, for there had been few winter lets and he said it was very seldom wanted at this time of year. However, kindling and logs had been left for the fire, and he hoped I should soon be fairly comfortable.

When I retrieved the keys from under a brick, and let myself in, the chill enveloped me at once, and it almost seemed warmer outside in the frost-charged day. Exploring the house did not take very long. It was functional, and its only characteristic touch was a pair of opposing high arched windows, one on the wall facing the road, the other facing the river. They had, I supposed, enabled the ferryman to watch for passengers. They let a great light into the main room of the place, even from the drawn winter sky, giving it a curious church-like quality, a sense of sanctuary, of radiance. I felt at once that it would do very well to dwell in during the day, as I pursued my studies. There were other relics of the place's past as a ferrykeeper's cottage—four rotting stumps on the bank, old mooring posts, and a pitted, scabbed brass bell by the side of the house, once used, I surmised, to summon the boatman's attention if he had not seen his passengers approach. A raggedy strand of hoar-encrusted rope hung down from the clapper.

Over the succeeding days I soon established the unvarying routine I prefer and which conduces, I claim, to the most concentration in pursuing obscure studies. In the morning, I would make myself a pan of porridge, sufficiently staunch to see me through until evening. Then I would take a brisk walk as far as I could across the Isle, becoming accustomed to its byways and channels, its rusting iron manufactories and machines, its hideous haciendas and pompous-porticoed new halls. Returning in the early noon, I would get a fire going, surly at first, later more eager, in the blackened grate, and settle down with my notebooks. By four o' clock it was quite dark and I felt myself snugger and securer still, a dweller in a far redoubt that none had need to disturb.

Though I thought I knew the Isle well from my previous visit and from the study of both ancient and modern maps, I found my morning walks often took me to curious corners or tracks that I had not encountered before, and which were unknown to the cartographers. Since the three great rivers and all their tributaries continue to shift their course when in spate, and since the people here seem pretty free to do what they want with the land, this did not surprise me too much. Yet there was one dismal plot which did puzzle me somewhat. It was some three days after Christmas, and I had gone far into the hinterland of the Isle, perhaps as remote from any settlement as it was possible to get there, for I always seek the furthest solitude possible.

Mostly the terrain is unvarying, and my way took me along straight dull tracks between flat fields holding only the dry husks of sapless stalks, or great turned clods of earth. Hungry crows wheeled in the dim white sky. At last, I came to a crossroads, of a kind: my thin, purposeless track carried on and further on, but it was intersected by an even more doubtful byway, merely an alley between great, clawing, overgrown bare hedges. No sign indicated where any of the four ways went. I was casting about to see if I could descry any landmark which might hint where I had got to, or where I might get to, when I noticed beyond the nameless track an unexpected hollow in the land.

Nowhere in the Isle has the pleasant undulations of some of our downland or shire country, and this sudden descent surprised me somewhat. I went nearer, and found it looked for all the world like a pit caused by quarrying—except that there is no quarrying here, and there was no sign of the loose rubble usually left behind at such sites. Further, this was no great excavation, but an open maw in the ground which could probably be descended, in a loping run, in a dozen or so strides. It would not be easy to accomplish, for there was barely any vegetation to offer a foothold. It was all ash-coated earth as if there had once, long ago, been some great fire here, and the dead cold embers had never yielded to the wind but clung instead to the sides of the pit.

Here, too, the crust of frost which had dissipated elsewhere in dank trickles of moisture as the weak sun rose, had retained its crystalline grip. I saw that once inside this sullen depression, it would be no easy matter to climb back up through the treacherous dust. I was about to resume my walk, when, taking a final look at the pit to see if there was any clue to its purpose, my attention was snagged by a stump at the very depth of the hollow. It was all but indistinguishable from the dreary bleached soil, except that it stuck out slightly like a dotard's back tooth from bony gums, ground down by the years. It put me in mind of the decaying mooring posts outside the ferry cottage and I involuntarily, for no intelligent reason whatever, looked to see if there were any more. And indeed I did soon see a second, even more sunken into the hard defile, and then, with a mounting sense of unease, a third and a fourth; and no more.

Well, it was a coincidence, and that was all—so I reassured myself. Old rotting wooden posts are to be found often enough in the country—the remains of a stockade, rubbing posts for cattle, gallows for crows, or simply marking out a plot of land. I chided myself for letting the place get the better of me, and, to shake off my subdued feeling, I picked up a nearby pebble, like an ossified egg, and sent it clattering down into the hollow where it bounced and jerked and—turned by some unseen obstruction—suddenly swerved and struck against one of the stumps. It was no art of mine that had achieved that, and I shrugged.

Yet as I resumed my former road I could not shake off the disquiet that had stolen upon me as I stared down into the pit at those four whittled stakes, driven down hard into the grim earth and weathered, perhaps by centuries, into gnarled relics.

That evening I stirred up the fire higher still than usual, and sat for a while meditating as the flames threw their benison upon my body and the shadows flickered over my face. My books and my notes lay to one side and I reflected again upon the curious history and mythology of the Isle, mulling over my growing conviction that some greater legend lay behind it all. I knew that lore may reach backwards as well as forwards, and take upon itself, in a new guise, all the potency of the past. Arthur, a Dark Age warrior, becomes also a Roman

Emperor and a medieval king. Robin Hood, a peasant outlaw, is transformed in retrospect as a pagan demi-god, and reinterpreted as a freedom fighter. That monkish chronicle of a great meteor's descent in the Dark Ages, for example, might be perfectly veridical in the essentials—embroidered a little, given a pious gloss, certainly, but the record of a true event. Looked upon later, though, it might be seen as the harbinger of some even greater doom or wyrd which was to befall the Isle.

As I crouched upon the flagstones before the hearth, dreamily turning over these things in my mind, I heard in the distance the sound of a furious drumming. I got up and tilted my head to one side, the way a creature does when it wants to listen more intently. The rapid pounding noise did not relent. I went to the great window that gave out onto the ferry road. I saw myself and the room reflected in the blackness beyond, and a glassy fire leaping. I turned off the electric light, and these images dimmed, letting through a vista of the road. There was a fine three-quarters moon, but it was harried by dark clouds, and threw only a pale, veiled light. I craned my gaze and made out a haze of dimness moving in the direction of the house, which my mind at once connected with the onset of the monotonous thudding. Despite the glow of the fire, I felt as if I was back in the room when I had first entered it, confronted by a slab of cold.

I could not draw away from the window. The sound became harder, heavier, faster, fiercer until I thought it was rising to a pitch I could not endure. And then there emerged, as the moon shrugged itself free of its sable assailants, a great burst of sudden light, which, however, only served to heighten and accentuate the aureole of darkness which massed around its edges.

Then there fell upon me a deep, harrowing, rivening surge, like pain or grief or shame. I had no understanding of its cause, nor of how it began or when it passed, but only that it bore in upon me and ran through all my thoughts and senses like fire or ice. And I felt overborn, as if by a measureless force that would fling aside any feeble attempts to resist.

That force, that cloud of darkness seemed to encompass the ferry house and all the terrain around, and I imagined it stalking across the whole Isle. For how long I stood transfixed by its presence, I could not say. But I know that it was followed by two simple, stark sounds, which struck me then as even more dreadful than the thundering clamour that had been raised before. One was the cracked clanging of a single bell: the other was of laughter, deep, full-throated and careless.

Both sounds echoed shrilly, and then receded in the brittle silence. Yet I seemed to listen to those echoes throughout most of the rest of the night, until dawn trickled into the sky with thin scarlet rivulets amid a great pallor of cloud.

As soon as the daybreak grew, I packed up my papers and my cases, placed the key back under the brick, and went to the station to wait for the earliest train. There was a chill wind and as I looked back, the bell was creaking and swaying, causing a dull tolling.

There were still a few days left of my time away, but I had not the will to go very far and so I made my way to the village of Allborough, perhaps a dozen miles beyond the river from Axholme. It looks out from its green bluff over the estuaries of the Don and the Trent and towards the broad waters of the Humber, and I gazed upon their slow silver waters for several hours, allowing the gentle, secluded atmosphere to restore me somewhat. Allborough is known for its great round medieval labyrinth, carved upon the turf, and carefully preserved by the village. After threading this quietly by myself, meditating as calmly as I could upon what I had heard and felt, a new heartening came upon me.

From the green maze, I went to the church, where a replica is laid out in tiles on the floor. It was growing dusk by now, and the door had just been locked for the night: but the churchwarden, whose house was opposite, saw me, and came out to let me in. He was an amiable and pottering sort of man, just the sort of harmless company I needed, and, peering from his thick glasses, he soon told me somewhat about himself and the village. He was not from these parts, but knew all about the local history, more so—he lightly implied—than those who had lived here much longer. He showed me the church's treasures, which included a Thompson admiralty clock with its vast pendulum, an eighteenth century bier, looking only like a hand-cart, and a Roman foundation stone concealed beneath a small trap door.

By a plain side altar, too, four shields were displayed. But instead of showing arms, they were all utterly black. "Those are Victorian," he said, "but we always put them out at this time of year." And then he asked if I knew that the nave had been restored by Becket's murderers, for the shields represented the suppressed emblems of the four assassins, and they were placed there on the eve before each 29 December, the anniversary of the saint's martyrdom in 1170.

For penance, he said, these knights had been ordered by the Pope to go to Jerusalem, then in Saracen hands, and expend their wealth upon the preservation of a church there. This they all took an oath to do. But, legend said, the assassins were more cynical, and more cunning, than that. For they had a ruse in mind. One of them knew that a part of the village of Allborough had always been called "Jerusalem", and so they came here. Until around 1690, the verger said, when it was stolen, a stone recorded their part in preserving the church. There was still today in the village, he averred, a house called Jerusalem Cottage; though it was quite modern, it was on the site of earlier buildings of that name.

If you look for them, you will find many legends of the Canterbury assassins, Reginald Fitzurse, Hugh de Moreville, William de Tracy, and Richard le Breton. The four cursed knights seem to have roamed throughout England, and left some sort of holy legacy wherever they went, in a vain attempt to atone for their infamous deed.

Yet one thing you will not find: their graves. They have no known tombs. By some it is said they did in the end journey to the real Jerusalem, and finish their days in vigil, fasting, and penance. They were buried, by this account, in some obscure monastery of the Crusader kingdom, or by the Templars in one of their citadels. Other traditions say that this was not so and only later piety, clerical inventions, credit them with such great expiation; in truth they never strayed far from England. No hallowed place would have their bones, nor did their families wish to have the taint of their relics upon them, so that when they each died, their bodies were taken to a remote place for secret, shameful burial. And several places now lay claim to that dishonour. But I think I would believe more in the truth of a place that does *not* claim them.

After all, perhaps Stevenson had only half of the matter. It is true there *are* places which stir the mind to think that a story must be told about them. But there are also, I believe, places which have their story stored already, and want to tell this to us, through whatever powers they can; through our legends and lore, through our rumours, and our rites. By its whispering fields and its murmuring waters, by the wailing of its winds and the groaning of its stones, by what it chants in darkness and the songs it sings in light, each place must reach out to us, to tell us, tell us what it holds.

The Fall of the King of Babylon

The thick dark water sucked greedily at the oars each time they dipped into the river's jaws, as if it was reluctant to let them go. He could tell by the way the boatman pushed hard against them that the current was offering him no help at all. It was as well that they did not have far to go. It was only a few minutes since they had left the banks of the city, and already the tall warehouses on the other side glowered above them. The towers of Babylon, he thought. Dark-bricked, dimly-lit on the bank side, with barred windows, and with foundations and lower chambers sunk deep in the ooze of the river, they were more like outgrowths than buildings.

The night was moonless and clouded, and the wind was riding in from the black marshes to the south. There had been heavy rain for days, and the river was broad and high, bloated. Its deep bed mud had been stirred up, and had darkened and soiled the waters. He sniffed at the rich, loamy miasma that had been released. The moisture in the air, squatting just above the water, seemed to stick to his face like grease, in silvery streaks.

They thudded against the old quay: it consisted of slabs streaked with green spittle like a sick man's tongue. There were a few great rusted iron rings, much bigger vessels than this had once tied up at the side. The boatman grunted and held the barque almost steady in the water, though still the river seemed to grip at it, as if it wanted to pull it under. His

113

passenger looked up at the dank wall: there was a narrow set of rungs, dripping with green weed and oily moisture. He swung himself out onto one of these, and caught hold of the cold rail. The boat began to move away at once. But its passenger was quicker. With a swift twist of his limbs, he kicked out, and caught the boatman a heavy blow on the head. He followed it with another. There was a baffled cry, and a gurgling of the waters as the boat thrashed about, out of control. Then there was a heavy crash and a great jet of the green water thrust upwards, flicking over him. He watched carefully, licking at the rank liquid on his face: little sparks of light glinted in his dark eyes. Nothing came to the surface. The boat began to drift away, empty. Good, he thought, I won't be needing you again anyway. Already he could feel his skin longing, and the river and its mud summoning him. Just a few more tide-hours, just a few.

He heaved: briefly, he was not sure he could haul himself up further without his soles or his fingers slipping, but he clung on and gasped to the top and onto the dank slabs, filling his breath with their ripe stench. Then he scrambled to his feet. He had business in Babylon.

છ

That was what they called it, this mudbank of a place, an island of sorts, a backwater within the Isle of Ely itself, cut off from the city when they diverted the river centuries ago.

It was a huddle of slimy buildings: the warehouses, twenty or so hovels, a few boatyards, the shed where they made osier baskets, and one pub. Some of its people were the ancestors of those who had always lived here, the original "exiles". The freemen beyond the water, that's what the city people had called them. Some of those families were still stubbornly clinging to the place. But most of the inhabitants had come later, drawn by its isolation, the way it was left alone, a law to itself, by the "mainland", as they sardonically called the city. And so Babylon had been built outwards onto the spit of mud, and upwards, with ramshackle attachments to the older structures: and there were also tunnels and archways between buildings, so that even here, necessary things could be carried on clandestinely.

And Babylon had a King, or that's what they called him. The boss. He liked the title. Elias Smith, his real name, it was said, but it didn't do to use it. He wasn't worried about a crown or a throne, but he did want the power, and the deference. Nothing moved on this mudbank without him knowing about it. Nobody lived there without paying his taxes, and those were set at whatever rate he pleased.

In the city there was a bishop and a soaring cathedral, with its great lantern tower, the glory of the Fens. But here in Babylon, there was no church, no chapel: just the eel warehouse, a ruined ziggurat of red bricks. And at its very top, in his own vaulted chamber, there resided the King. You had to be conducted there: no set of stairs led straight to it. There were different iron flights for each floor, and linking corridors, and empty halls, which you were hustled through in a blur. You went back, if you went back, a different way. But rumour said that from a concealed door in the King's reception room, there was a chute, a steep chute that went down, down, straight into the Great Ouse. And at such force that nothing sent down ever surfaced again.

In the warehouse, above smouldering pits of slow-burning alder-wood, skinned silver eels were being smoked in long rows of round gallows like dark chandeliers. The columns of flesh swayed and twisted in the draughts, as if they were still alive. There was an acrid smell from the embers and also, still, the deep dank odour of river mud, not yet burnt out of the bodies of the eels. The two together were almost overpowering. In the cellars, frequently flooded, and always dripping with damp and mould, were the slabs where the catch was first reamed of its gleaming skin. A streaked tin tub of eel heads stood in one corner: the black eyes still glinted in the dim light.

The King of Babylon owed a vast wealth to this gruesome river harvest. But he was restless this night. There was something wrong in his realm, he knew that, and although he could not say exactly what, there were signs. There hadn't been a catch in days. The women in the weaving-sheds were murmuring amongst themselves: they shut up too quickly when they saw him. The river was too solid: he did not like the look of it. And from over in the city, there was too much talk of a foreigner seen, staring across at Babylon, asking questions. He had a strangeness in his tongue, the King's spies said, and probably came from beyond the seas.

The King's heavy form paced about his high room, and he glared down from this eyrie to the darkened alleys and empty yards below, through the small panes of smeared grey glass. Like the bricks of his building, his face and hands were a blackened red. Abruptly, he turned away, and tugged at a bell-rope. A cracked clangour sounded. Boot-steps stumped in the stairwells and along the corridors. A young woman, with cropped hair, and dressed in rough black clothes, presented herself. She had a white scar on her left cheek. It gleamed silver in a face already a dirty pale, the colour of congealed candle-wax.

He stared at her. She lowered her dark eyes, and fidgeted.

"Who's in Babylon tonight?"

"Forty-two souls, sir. Eighteen down below, doin' the skinnin', smokin', and saltin'. Balin, patrollin' the building, with Den and Pulver. Twelve in *The Anchor*: that's nine o' the fishing men, the potman, the barmaid, old Agar talking to 'imself. Then there's Mother Shearn in her cottage . . . "

"What's she doing?"

"Playin' at cards, sir."

"Playing? Or reading them?"

"Couldn't tell, sir. Looked like playin' though. She didn't have that funny look in her eyes."

But you do, the King thought, that's why you won't look in mine. Hiding something. He gestured to her to go on.

"Four o' the women in the basket shed. And then there's them two men you put on the wharves, lookin' out. That you didn't tell me, nor nobody about. But I spotted 'em. And then me, and you, see, sir, makes forty-two. "

He grunted. "Been everywhere?"

"Everywhere."

"Would you like to be skinned, Nix?"

Still she would not look at him.

"I have been everywhere," she repeated, slowly.

"Skinned, salted, smoked alive on one of the eel-gallows?"

"Everywhere," she murmured.

∞

Mother Shearn did not tarry long in the brick hovel she called her home, where dirty lace tried to escape through cracks in the smeared windows. After she saw Nix's pale face glimmer in the grey panes, then vanish, she blew out the candle. She continued to count out the cards in their rows and columns, knowing them by touch in the gloom. She had been in Babylon longer than anyone remembered, and was rumoured to be the only one on the isle that King Elias was afraid of; wisely, perhaps, she had never put this to any great test. Her face was silted and brown like the river's leavings.

She hunched over the cards for some time, then hastily gathered them up and stuffed them in a little pouch of frayed red satin, which hung from the thick leather belt at her waist. She wrapped a bundle of tawny shawls around her shoulders. Outside, she sniffed the dank night air. Her thick greasy nostrils seemed to suck in and sift the stench. Then she made a gurgling noise at the back of her throat, and shuffled towards *The Anchor*. Its door unleashed a babble, then swung closed behind her.

Old Agar was reciting to himself from the Bible again: he seldom did anything else. At least, it sounded like the Bible. There was a lot of muttering about the things to come. He barely registered her arrival.

A group of men in the corner looked up from their beer as she moved towards them. She thrust her face into their hoarse-throated circle.

"Eels is risin'," she said, quietly.

They fell silent for a few moments then started to mutter.

"Can't be."

"Naw, not tonight, Mother."

"Have another look at they cards o' yours."

"Get her a gin."

"Eels is risin'," she repeated.

Reluctantly they began to get to their feet, clumsily lace up the boots they'd eased loose, and climb into heavy, soil-streaked coats, gather up kit bags. From a corner, they took up nets, clubs and the shining gleaves, long, speared forks, like primitive weapons. Grumbling and spitting, they headed for the door.

She watched them go, and then signalled with a quick jerk of her head for a double genever. She felt the spirit graze her throat. Yes, they were rising, all right, swimming up from the silt and the mud, following some instinct old and blind. She knew that: she always did; whatever the instinct was, she could catch its dim echoes, like a coiling of green miasma in her mind. But this time there was something else she could not fathom. There was a cold gap. She could not tell when the rising would end, when they would return to the slime, to the river's depths. She shivered, drew her shawls closer about her, and signalled for another spirit.

ℰℭ

The men trudged, then waded, down to the shallows where the boats were kept. They lurched and jostled against each other. They could already tell the hag was right: the smell in the air was heavy enough to get through the beer in their heads. They bundled the eel-tools in a pile on the mudbank and hauled the boats toward them on their sodden ropes. The brown slime stuck to their hands. The coracles seemed heavy in the swollen waters, reluctant to respond. They heaved harder, their boots sinking into the clinging clay. At last, with a jolt and a surge, the dank wooden shells began to move towards them. Ben Crawke got his in first, but the sudden impetus took him by surprise and when the boat bumped against his shins, his fuddled brain wasn't quick enough to react, and he toppled forward into the bottom of the boat. Cackles of laughter greeted his mishap, and were redoubled when Crawke screeched. The boat thrashed about in the water and in the dim light they could see his limbs flailing about comically. Why didn't he steady himself? He used to be able to hold his drink better than that. Still, it was worth watching. After they'd let him mess about for a few moments, still bellowing fit to burst the moon, one of the men stooped down quickly and caught up the trailing boat-rope, and another helped to try to steady the juddering. It took both of them to tug the boat back once again to the bank. And then Crawke's head emerged.

The youngest fisher, Thom, had been sent against his will to an elementary school in the city for a year or two, before he slipped away back to Babylon, where they didn't come looking for him again. One day he had been shown a book of myths which he quite liked because it had a lot of pictures of strange things in it, things that even Babylon did not possess. And one of these was of a woman with a head all covered in snakes.

Crawke looked like that now. Except they weren't snakes. They were eels. And they weren't just in his hair, like that woman's. They were on his face too. No, not just on his face; in it. Some of the men stumbled forward, as if they could help, seizing their clubs and the long barbed spears. Then the river current, which had been slow and sluggish, seemed to give a great surge, to rise up in a sudden swell, and the ropes dropped slack as the rest of the boats rushed to the bank. And then they saw the writhing within them, a great mass of the dark coiling creatures. It would have been the greatest haul ever made, something to boast about in *The Anchor* for years to come. Except that it was all wrong: for the first, and last, time in their lives, they had no need to go out for the catch. It had come to them.

The river surged again, lunging at them. The strong waters sucked at their limbs. They tried to ground their boots in the mud, to grab hold of the mooring posts, even to clutch at the sharp, yellow-green reeds. Still, they were summoned into the depths. And when they finally gave way, they found out why the current was so fierce. It wasn't just the water that had sucked them under.

∞

Nix crouched in a dark corner. She had five dark corners on the isle where she could go and hide. To get to this one, she had quietly moved aside a huddle of osier baskets, then a stretch of oilcloth, revealing an iron lid. This she forced up with a little knife she'd filched once from one of the fishermen: it had grey string round the handle for better grip. The blade dislodged the seal of grit and mud around the lid, and she heaved it up. Below was a narrow rung, and at the bottom of this a platform above a black channel of water. It ran under the warehouse and came out under one of the unused cellars. Even Elias did not know about this. When she was alone she did not call him the King, even though she belonged to him. She rubbed the scar on her white face.

They told her she had been born in Babylon, and so she belonged to him. There wasn't anybody else claiming her; that was for sure. But she did not call him the King because she knew, somewhere inside her, that there was another ruler of this isle, and always had been, and he would come again. Maybe somebody had told her a story about it once, maybe she had overheard a few things and put them together, maybe she had always known it. But she was more certain of it even than the breath of the boss, Elias, when he took hold of her and pulled her close and stared at her. That breath was the thing she feared the most, because she could tell from it what would happen next. His breath, heavy, rotten, rank, seemed to enter her like poison. And then his venom worked in her veins, all the way through her. But when she later lay quivering, trying to secrete the poison, trying to get rid of it, she also called, far in the depths of her mind, called and sang—to the unknown King, to the one that she knew would one day hear her.

Her body in its black clothes tautened, so tight, so intense she thought it might suddenly change, in a flicker, into something else. Footsteps. Coming steadily towards her. Heavy, too, sending echoes into the tunnel. His? Elias? She felt something surge in her, a burst of hot defiance. Her fingers tightened on the corded handle.

&

He could feel the waters rising. Already they would be filling up the underground channels, surging into the vaulted chambers, clawing at the walls. The deep, dark stench of the water called to him: already he had offered it two bodies he'd found prowling about after him. They'd been distracted by some babbling young fisher-boy, who clung on to them, shouting about a face he'd seen, a face that was writhing. The boy would have more to talk about now.

But there was a greater urging in him too, more overpowering than the river. He knew she was here: the sense coursed in his limbs like a shot of silver. He waited. Then his eyes seemed to form the image of an iron disk, and draw his body towards the shadow of the warehouse with insistent force.

℘

She heard the grating noise, saw the lid rise up. A face of white shone in the gloom, and then a form slid easily down and dropped beside her. She felt her body become even more tense. And then stared at his black eyes, stared hard, and saw her own reflected back. She was seized and thrust into the dark waters. They closed about her head. For a few moments she was blinded and numb. Then she kicked out, thrust herself forward, and at once felt her body become part of the current. Around her, forms moved in the water.

When they emerged into the cellar, her breath was soiled at once by the burning smell from the smoking gallows above them in the building, which seemed to permeate every streaked brick. She felt a plunge of fear, and she wanted to cry out. But then a hard rage seethed through her and her eyes gleamed in hatred.

Her companion touched her, and beckoned. Their dark, dripping forms moved lithely to a stair and quickly ascended. Flight followed flight, in a crooked route through

122

corridors that glistened as they left behind them a trail of the black slime.

And there was his door. Behind it, the man who liked to be called the King of Babylon. Now the hatred was so fierce in her that she knew it would change her forever: her body could not contain that dark fire. She heard the bell shout for her from its bronze throat: she heard that name bawled, "Nix! Nix!"; she heard the threats that followed. Her fingers felt the silver scar upon her face. Her companion thrust her to the stone floor, and crouched beside her. Then, together, as if they were one being, they lunged, and burst through the door. There was a sharp, keening sound, and a barbed glieve thrust through the air toward them. They twisted with a wild instinct, and it clanged uselessly aside. It was raised again for another strike, but stopped: it was held before them, holding them at bay. But still within them, they felt that instinct surging strong.

Then the King saw the intruders' faces change. They seemed to pulse rapidly, to quicken and writhe before him. And the flesh began to turn colour. It had been white, like the skinned strips dangling from the gallows below. Now it was darkening, becoming brown, like the river water, rank green, like its weed, and finally black, black like its depths of mud. And the shape of their faces was changing too: becoming sleek, sharp, pointed; until at last he knew exactly what he faced, and stared into the utter glinting dark of the eyes.

Elias Smith, alias The King of Babylon, bellowed, and backed quickly into an ante-chamber. He spun an iron wheel in the corner of the outer wall. With a grating noise, a door swung heavily open. There was a large arched tunnel, like an open mouth, with a brick throat, sloping steeply down. He leapt into its maw, skimming its streaked surface, feeling the fetid air rising to fill his breath as he descended at reckless speed. Behind, he could sense the things slithering even faster after him.

The Other Salt

By the time the train, with its two rusting carriages, had made its way along the causeway to the halt, Étienne was the last passenger left. The journey had been a long one, and in the hour that had just passed, the country had seemed desolate, unvarying. The terrain was flat, relieved only by a few stark, weeping trees, or tussocks of thin grass. The ground seemed heavy, soaked in the acrid water that gathered in dank pools or reluctantly oozed along dug channels. Through the cracks and gaps in the windows, the pervading odour emanated into the coach, and in the dim light through the smeared glass lamps, Étienne began to think the stench was almost visible, uncoiling itself in the gloom. He gripped the handle of his valise firmly, and felt carefully in his pocket for the slender silver vial it held.

At last, with a dull mumbling, the train came to a stop. The halt was no more than two wooden platforms, and a shack that was the only shelter. In the dusk, his eyes dimmed by the subdued light inside the carriage, Étienne searched for a figure. Some piece of the twilight seemed to detach itself from the shape of the shed, so the passenger got out of the train, which was sighing to itself, and walked, with a certain hesitation, towards this form. As he drew closer, the pallor of a face flickered from out of a drab column of clothes: a thick woollen muffler, ragged jacket, billowed trousers, square-toed boots.

"M. Frank? Let me take your case." The boy's accent, even in those few words of greeting, unconsciously conveyed the rich patois of this far corner of the country, the soft consonants and long, echoing vowels. "It is not far: will you walk?" And Étienne Frank nodded briefly. A few steps of sodden wood led down from the platform and onto a track, raised on a swollen bank above the marsh. It had once been given a coat of asphalt, but that had been bitten away by the lapping waters and the scouring winds. Grass clumps, gravel, and lumpy patches of repair took its place. The rank odours of the night rose up from the great expanse of mud, water, and soaked timber that surrounded them: the loamy smell filled his breath and he coughed. It was said that this was one of the last unaltered, untreated enclaves left; that all attempts to drain it had failed, or faltered, leaving the sagging relics of broken pumps to rust away, which only added to the bleakness of the terrain. Just enough was done to prevent complete inundation when the rains were heaviest, or the sea raged furthest inland; banks and dikes were meagrely maintained, and a few machine plants kept going, but this was a truce at best against the true nature of the country, the waterlogged wastes.

The boy seized Étienne's arm and held him back just as he was about to place his foot in a crumbling pit on the edge of the track. "We will soon be there," he said, with the slightest tint of reproach for his guest's inattention. A waterfowl's plaintive call echoed across the dimness. Étienne began to sense some other taste in the air, more elusive than the dank loam, which did not quite suffocate it; perhaps the night scent of some wayside flower. It was sweet, yet brittle, and he found himself breathing in quickly to try to sift it in his nostrils and even, as it seemed, take it upon his tongue. He was about to ask the boy about it, when their steps took them around a curve in the track, and a pane of gold shone out at them. Around it, the black bars of unfastened shutters, and the subdued lustre of old brick walls, with a starlit glint upon the reed roof, revealed the outlines of the remote house where Étienne was to make his stay. Their tread upon the track must have sounded in the silence, for the narrow door swung open, and a face briefly appeared. "My sister, Jeanne," said the boy, who evidently then remembered that he had not introduced himself; "and I am Alain. We have a broth ready, and your room is all arranged."

Étienne murmured thanks, but in truth his attention was elsewhere, still craning after the elusive, keen fragrance carried on the night air.

It had been hard to find any place to stay so deep in the sea-marsh country. The nearest hotel was far beyond, on the fresher littoral where only limpid streams ran; the closest farmhouse was on the pastures that at last heaved themselves free of the waters in the undulating champaign that bordered the wastes. Only by talking to some of the old retired water engineers had he learned of a few addresses of inhabitants who might take in a boarder, because they would want the money to supplement the grudging living from the land. Most of his letters had elicited no reply: but the young woman Jeanne had written to him briefly to say that he might stay with her and her brother for a season, if he did not mind simple food and board. They had not asked why he wanted to come, and he murmured only of local history research, as they conversed haltingly over the stew, taken by lamplight on a coarse, bowed table, the rays illuminating the grain and the knots of the simply planed wood. And illuminating, too, the pale, austere faces of Jeanne and Alain, anxious that he should be pleased, but quietly defiant too, since he was in their house. Étienne spoke as pleasantly as he could of his journey, of his one previous visit here, as a student, and of the water engineer, old Phillippe, who had introduced them. But still a part of him was abstracted, chasing his memory of the tang in the air that he had briefly and elusively sensed: and he knew too that there was a reticence, a reserve in his hosts, almost as difficult to define, yet assuredly present.

His room was reached by an attic stair, and was dominated by a great oak bed, with a patterned counterpane in rich reds and yellows, all the colours that the land seldom saw, except perhaps in a sunset glinting in a pool, or in a few apples coaxed from dampened trees that had seen just enough of the sunlight. He sat on the edge of the bed and took out from his jacket pocket the slender silver tube. Tilting it to the glass lamp, he peered inside. At the rounded base, a few grains caught the light. He held the vessel to his nose. But the deep loam smell was in the bricks and the timbers of the cottage and he could discern nothing else, not even the faint lilt of that rarer aroma he had found on the road.

It was the vial, or what it contained, that had brought him here, and still he did not know if he was in calm pursuit of a discovery in the natural sciences, or only following the faint spoor of an old legend. In the cold damp of the room, in the middle of this desolate mire, far from the amenities of the city where he had studied, he felt most the futility of his journey, and succumbed to the sullen lappings of a tide of melancholy.

The "other salt", that was what he was here to find, if it existed. A different salt that old chroniclers mentioned respectfully in their accounts of the richest banquets, that some shipowner's accounts listed in minute, but costly, quantities; that a few dandies of the Second Empire claimed to use to coat the mouthpieces of their amber or jade ciga-rette-holders, to infuse the fumes they drew; the "other salt", rarer than all the spices of the East, than cardamom from Bhutan, Zanzibar cloves, Coromandel ginger, or the blue pepper that only the Parsee traded.

By careful study of all the accounts, by mapping changes in ships' manifests, by tracking the routes of pedlars, by the fragmentary, scorched chronicles of abbeys and priories in the region, Étienne Frank believed that he had discerned a pattern and that here, in this desolate hinterland of the Atlantic coast, might be found one of the last sanctuaries of the "other salt". With such a hope he fortified himself for sleep: the journey had tired him and he soon sank into a heavy torpor.

Over the following days, the pattern of his existence was the same. He would rise early, with the inhabitants of the house, take a breakfast of the coarse bread and musty goat's cheese, sometimes with a spoon of honey or a small wrinkled apple, and with plenty of coffee, and go out to walk the track and gaze across the expanse of the mire, each time filled anew with the futility of his quest. For he hardly knew what he expected to find, in what form the secret of the other salt might be revealed to him. Such a trade, even if it had been of the smallest proportions, must have left some trace on the terrain: perhaps a round bank where a primitive distillation vat had been made; or a rim of a stone chest where the rare salt had been stored under heavy slabs; or the thin traces of a path to no obvious place, possibly revealing the route to the source. Tentatively, he took some of the smaller trails, goat tracks at most, that led from the one true way, despite a grave warning from Alain not to stray far from the embanked road, which alone held firm against the treachery of the marsh.

Each evening he would return dispirited: he had begun to form a picture of the obscure land in his mind, but he was no nearer any clue to the salt he thought that it harboured. Over their evening meal, a variation on the broth he had been given on his first day, he thought that Jeanne or Alain were beginning to regard him with a wary pity, and they hinted that they knew what he was seeking. Under the lamp, the angular purity of their white faces was thrown into sharp relief, and the spell of colour in their brown eyes, in their hair with the gleaming sheen of dank wood, and in their tentative lips, became wonderfully familiar to him, and would refresh his spirits at the day's end. Though he had not definitely sensed again the strange sweet tang he had caught on the roadside on his first day, he thought that sometimes a hint of it arose when the girl served his broth, her pale hands deftly plying the ladle into the deep earthenware bowls: he wondered if it might be some herb they used.

The duration of his visit began to draw to a close and his wanderings became more frankly aimless, and a little riskier. He realised that he was drawn to the atmosphere, the miasma of the marshes, that strange mingling of the heavy earth, the encroachments of the last thin rivulets of the sea, the pools and pits of brackish rainwater, and the few tough weeds and black trees. The long pale horizon held him, too, unbroken by any tower or high building, barely serrated by the few iron ghosts of the old pumps. As far as his gaze would go, he saw purely a dark plane, in which only the glinting of the waters and the stiff persistence of the grasses made any indentation. Sometimes he would think he could descry some past sign of human habitation, a track or a huddle of stones, and would at hazard make a cautious, stumbling way towards it, only to find as he drew nearer that he was seeing only a chance natural alignment of stones. Once he thought he saw a tall carved menhir rising from the ground, such as may be found in Breton graveyards, and was exultant at this sign of ancient settlement: but, on drawing nearer, he found he had been deceived by a stark, stripped tree. There was no cemetery in the marshland, it seemed: the only road must also be a coffin path, to the church far beyond.

On the last day of his stay, he said at breakfast that he was going to try to head further across the waste towards the sea, into the terrain he had not yet seen: he thought he now knew a network of narrow alleys that would take him there. Jeanne's hand darted to rest briefly upon his in a delicate gesture of restraint, and Alain too murmured caution. But he was determined, and set off with a new sense of purpose, stepping confidently along the goat paths, which seemed to him quite well-defined, if labyrinthine in their direction, towards the faint line of grey where the inlet of the sea and the last shudderings of the waterland met. At times he caught the sense once again of the faint fragrance from that flower, or herb, or whatever it was, that had floated into his breath on his first day. The heavy stench of the damp earth seemed to recede as he strode, leaving space for the keener air from the lapping rivulets that became fresher as they surged towards the sea, and which rippled in a succession of curved shapes, like the repeated glinting of silver scythes. He raised his eyes and thought he could discern the strand where the grasses at last gave out completely to the shore.

A few minutes more, and he stood on bare wet crystalline sand, taut as flesh. He surveyed the whole of the inlet, the sharp streams licking at the shore, and the last haggard, stubborn wiry vegetation clinging to a few clods of soil, their leaves coated with grains of the fine sand.

Here it was almost possible to believe in the sullen beauty of the Marais Gat, that its detractors, who avoided it for the gentler coast or the soft pastures beyond, were wrong, were limited in their perception, were lulled by the obvious. And yet, for all that, even here, where the air was clearest, where the morass retreated, he still felt a sense of overwhelming melancholy, a deep, bleak sadness. It was not simply that he had failed in his search for some sign of the old salt workings, nor that this was his last day in the region: it felt more like some exhalation of the country itself, some ancient echo of its soul.

That night, in his attic room, he went over and over his notes, the sources, the conclusions he had reached, and remained more convinced than ever that all the tales, the chronicles, even the dry lading lists of ships, and merchants' account books, suggested that it was here where the "other salt" was to be found. And yet he was convinced not a trace of the trade remained. How could this be?

In the morning, breakfast with Jeanne and Alain was subdued, broken only by painfully light conversation. He had come to like them, and to respect their quiet, reticent life, and he hoped they returned this fragile fondness too. He stood at the door with his case by his side, and they both faced him awkwardly, arms by their sides. Their pale forms seemed at once so vulnerable to him that impulsively he reached out, and brushed his lips on the side of each face in turn. Then he stepped back. A pang of a bright, bitter, powerful taste pervaded him, and quickly his fingers went to his mouth. As he stared at the brother and sister, he could not stop the tip of his tongue running over and over his lips, so that he should know more of the strange, sweet but sharp tang. It was like the aroma that had entered his spirit when he first came to the marsh, when the boy had seized his arm to stop him stumbling; it was like the tint of rare essence that had emanated when the girl had leant towards him to serve his evening broth. But it was stronger, richer by far than these, and he understood, with a deep sensual knowledge, why this curious spice had been so prized.

And then, in a surge of understanding, he knew the source of the "other salt", and his mind leapt on before he could stop himself, to further terrible speculations; he *knew* now why there was no visible sign remaining of the workings for this exquisite mineral; he could surmise at once why the marshes were still so uninhabited; he sensed why a mournfulness haunted the shore, where the ships had once come; and—but here his thoughts stopped short, and he stared at the pale figures before him. He could not, would not, think what memory they kept of how precisely the precious pale crystals had once been harvested.

Three Odd Societies

The Tontine of Thirteen

It was a bleak winter's noon on the Westmorland fells. Robert Lorne had been walking the stony track for over an hour without seeing a single soul. Nor had there been any sign of a house which still had inhabitants. There were hollow shells, roofless and assailed by skeletal shrubs and creepers, but on the bare hills there was apparently no human figure, nor much sign of the human hand to be seen. He liked it that way: it was why he had come here. For the last few months, he had been dutifully cataloguing a library to be sold at auction, the "property of a gentleman", except that some of the contents suggested the late owner had not always been *quite* the gentleman. Now, he wanted to be out in the emptiness.

As he walked, however, there came to his hearing a faint, curious sound. At first he paid it no attention, and it hovered on the edge of his consciousness, but it seemed very slowly to gain upon him and to insist that he listen. He could not place what it could be. It was not birdsong; it was not a singing in the wires; it was not the wail of a gate upon its hinges. Yet it had something of all those, a jingling, metallic, rippling quality. He paused in the road and looked around him. Up ahead, where the track dipped, there was an inlet on the bald terrain, a plot of land fenced off from the rest, with a sort of cultivation to it, though he could not make out exactly what. Trees neater than the haggard thorns and thin pale birches of the fells had been planted there, tall evergreens which were like ink strokes upon the parchment sky. But that was not the direction of the ringing sound he could now increasingly sense. He turned fully and looked behind him at the way he had been.

In the dim day, in the pale, drawn light, there seemed to move a distant darkness. He had the thought that this was why the land around was so wan: all there was of depth, of rich, royal black, had been leached away so that it might be gathered in the train or entourage of what was coming towards him. He craned his gaze to try to see more and tried to make sense still of the ringing sound, which now seemed to have beneath it a dull rumbling slow thunder. At first what he saw was merely mass, a cloud of black, and movement, a steady, unvarying progress towards where he stood. He could not imagine what it could be, but felt apprehensive and vulnerable simply standing there, as if he were waiting for a dark wave to engulf him. So he turned again and quickened his stride, heading for the little enclosure he had seen.

As he came up to this, with the ringing and rumbling noises gaining in force behind him, he saw the narrow green plot for what it was: a country graveyard. There was a simple wicket gate and above this two curved iron stems met at a glass lantern. A single, crumbling, mossy path led straight from this and on either side were a few monuments: perhaps about a dozen, though he did not pause to count exactly. It was hardly surprising the burial place was so sparsely occupied, given its remoteness; indeed, it seemed a contrary place for it at all, with no house or farm in sight, still less anything that might be called a settlement. But some places, and some old sects, he knew, were apt to inter their dead at a distance, or had once been obliged to, so as to elude official disapproval. No doubt this was one such. He became curious to know a little more, but there was no sign or notice board, not even the customary request to walk respectfully or to remove dead flowers. There were, indeed, no flowers of any kind here, dead or otherwise: only monuments in stone the colour of winter cloud, as if something of the drear day had been caught, solidified and sculpted into their stark shapes; obelisks, columns, rugged rough spheres of rock, draped urns or low plain tablets. Neither were there, he realised, any crosses, and no angels. A severe sect, then, not given to images. There was, however, one open, oblong slot in the grey earth, its sides glistening in the dank day. He passed it quickly, and did not look too closely inside, he could not quite say why: perhaps it did not seem right, or perhaps it did not seem advisable, a taboo thing to do.

At the furthest end of the little burial ground there was an iron seat, black with damp and red with rust, and almost overgrown by a weeping laburnum, itself streaked with a green spittle of decay. The tree formed a bare arch over the bench. He made his way to this, both to rest and to await the passing of whatever it was that was surging up the road towards him. The noise of that grew in intensity and the low monotonous thunder began to become predominant until it was clear enough for him to recognise: it was the sound of horses' hooves, and quite a number of them, and of carriage wheels, and within those the jingling of the harnesses.

Soon there came into view four fine plumed horses pulling a gleaming black phaeton of silver, brass, and polished paintwork. Solemnly it drew up to the little gate and stopped. And then, one by one, further carriages followed, with one or with two horses at their helm, each drawing up either beyond or behind the first to arrive. These were a motley assembly, from simple gigs and traps to a semi-brougham and even an old city growler, but each was thoroughly burnished and bedecked with black ribbons.

Robert Lorne knew that it would be seemly to remove himself. But already four top-hatted and frock-coated pallbearers were steadying their load upon their shoulders and positioning themselves to process through the entrance. He could hardly walk down the only path towards them. He looked over the wall of the churchyard, and saw spiny gorse bushes and a deep drop: there was no escape there. And these thoughts were half-hearted anyway: for really, he knew he wanted to watch the ceremony. So he shrank back further into the gloom afforded by the laburnum and hoped he would be ignored by the mourners.

Yet in fact, he soon saw, that would be an exaggeration. The four pallbearers, professional funeral men he could plainly see by their stolidity and solemn ease of practice with their burden, were followed by but one man, equally impeccably attired but just as plainly apart from them. Beneath the tall hat was a wrack of a man, lean and stooping, with hanks of wild white hair reaching their brittle fingers over the forehead and cheekbones of a narrow face. Lorne found it hard not to stare at the man, but forced himself to look beyond him in search of the priest and those others who had taken the procession of horse-drawn vehicles here, who were, he supposed, giving the first mourner a proper precedence. But none came. The horses could be heard to stamp, and snuffle, their drivers to murmur, the harnesses quietly to ring. But no other human figure descended from the carriages.

The pallbearers halted at the open earthen niche and lowered the chest they had carried into position. The old man muttered a passage, hurriedly, reluctantly. The cords tautened, were lowered, and then retrieved with a slither. The four men marched solemnly away, each curtly raising his hands to the brim of his shiny hat. The sole mourner did not bestow a single glance below but directed his gaze outwards. Then he beckoned Lorne over.

"You are trespassing, sir. Not, I will admit, upon grief. But upon a private burial ground. No matter. Accompany me.

Blanch, by the way. Uchtred Blanch." Robert Lorne gave a slight start: surely not . . . but he recovered his courtesy at once, and gave his own name in return. But his attempt to apologise, and to explain that he had his own destination, was brushed aside. "Nonsense. Walking, you say? Time your own. You will join me for the funeral meats. Can't refuse."

And Lorne saw that he couldn't. It was not simply that he felt an obligation since he had intruded himself, and a deference to so solitary an elderly gentleman; not only these very proper instincts of civility and decorum, but also that Mr. Blanch's manner admitted of no contradiction. And so he rode with the solitary mourner, who had now fallen silent, in the most well-appointed of the carriages, conscious of his own rough and threadbare clothing by comparison with the seemly attire of his host.

The equipage took a narrow rutted lane off the road over the fells and drew up at a solitary house, Georgian in its dimensions, yet lacking the grace that style usually gave. It was coated in a drab stucco, perhaps once white, but which had now absorbed a greyness and even a vile unhealthy faint blue. The tall windows hardly seemed to have more light in them than the walls. Mr. Blanch ushered him in and cast his hat and gloves upon a little table, then pushed open a door. A surly fire muttered in the corner; to one side a table had been set with cold food and a decanter. The room, it seemed to Lorne, was correctly furnished, and yet nothing in it had character, as if its appointments would exist just as indifferently whether there was anybody there or not.

"You are no doubt curious," Blanch began, between meagre peckings at the food before him, "to know more about the scene you chanced to witness. And I am ready to tell you. Why not? It is so seldom I have company here, I should scarcely spurn it when it presents itself, as you have done. *Proper* company, I mean."

Lorne was uncertain what the qualification implied. Perhaps the pale old man excluded servants or tradespeople—he was old-fashioned enough for that—or perhaps there was other "company" that he did not welcome.

"You have witnessed, you see, the last-but-one, or perhaps the last, of a particular ritual. Yes, a very particular ritual. When we started, we were all about the same age, give or take a few quarterings of the moon. And that was an age when the provoking of elders and the usurping of custom seemed the very things to do, you see? We were young, flippant I dare say, satirical anyway. And we started a Thirteen Club whose dinners were marked both by the flouting of superstitions and, I may say, a cavalier contempt for good form and proper order. Salt was liberally spilled, knives crossed, the port passed the wrong way, smoking was permitted at any stage, we got up and wandered around whenever we felt like it, and reached across the table to seize any dishes we wanted, without asking for them to be passed. It will seem very tame stuff to you now, I expect. But then, why, we thought we were the very heathens.

"If I ever knew whose idea the pact was, I have long forgotten, in the sixty years and more that have elapsed since. But its elaboration was surely the work of us all, arguing and throwing in ideas as we dined so unconventionally. Eventually, and solemnly, its final form was all worked out, and written down, and we all signed it with a flourish in the vilest, vividest ink we could find. The scroll still has those signatures, faded now (for the ink really was bad) in dim scarlet, green, purple, ochre.

"In its essence, it was a simple form of tontine. You are familiar with the term? Yes, indeed. We were each to undertake to meet once a year for dinner on the Eve of St. Lazarus, and to subscribe a sum to a fund. A burial ground for our exclusive use was to be purchased as soon as the fund was capable of this. Why, then we were all freethinkers, pagans, atheists, and decadents, and wanted some plot where the most curious monuments could be raised without demur. Once this was found, and the time came for one of us to die, all the others left were to be sure to attend the obsequies, each in a black coach drawn by a pair of black steeds, fully caparisoned and plumed. That was our *aesthetical* instinct, you see. For each one who had gone before, the fund was to be used to commission the same equipage on their behalf, so that there would always be twelve following carriages, one for each of us.

"When the deed of tontine was drawn up, it must have seemed that I was the least likely of all to be the last survivor. My flesh, you see, as they often taunted me, was a sort of absinthe-green, and my form then was frail. I stooped like the pale lilies that lolled in my rooms, and my eyes were like a pair of guttering candles. Perhaps, young man, you might be thinking I have reverted to that condition?"

Lorne managed a non-committal murmur.

"Well, you need not say so. Sixty and more years have elapsed since that time. But my appearance then, in any case, belied my industry. I had determined that I would carry on my spurning of the suburban into literature, the one great talent I thought I had. I saw—am I mistaken?—that when I introduced myself, there was a slight start of recognition from you? Then, sir, you are a savant of strange, forgotten literature, that I can tell. For you are correct. I was the author then of one slim 'shocker', as they were called in those days. It was cheaply done in card wrappers, true enough, but I regarded it with a certain prideful relish: *Dr. Saprophyte*. Yes, you know it. Oh, I have written other books since then, but none so precious to me, or, indeed to collectors. The villain of my novel was made of flourishing but unprepossessing soft dun flesh, and seemed to thrive in the vicinity of invalids and the newly dead. He was ever a haunter of accidents, battlefields, cemeteries. A modern ghoul, in short. It was impossible to convict him of any crime, and yet staunch men had their suspicions. When at length—rather to my reluctance—he is slain, the grim-jawed vigilantes are horrified to see his body disintegrate into thousands of foul floating flakes. What became of these seeds was the subject, of course, of my sequel, *Spore of Saprophyte*: and then I wrote several more."

He gestured vaguely towards a long, a very long row of dull spines.

"Several", Lorne knew, was putting it mildly. The series was one of the longest-running in popular literature. The titles did not improve with persistence. Even his publishers, despite the early successes, had cried for mercy in the end.

"The Great War, of course, in which I was naturally unfit to serve, as could plainly be seen, somewhat aided my chances. Four of the thirteen of us perished there. My own strength grew, though, and I was able to live comfortably from the sales of my *shockers*, which soon spread throughout the world, and were known in many tongues. Each year when we met I was able to hear of the vicissitudes of my fellows, who all encountered the general tragedies and afflictions that are our common lot: except mine, you see. For I kept to my study, saw only my attendants, wrote on and on, and enjoyed the lush fruits of my labours. I saw that they envied me, and perhaps our gatherings were not always quite as cordial as in the days of our youth, but we stuck to them, every Eve of St. Lazarus. Indeed, I started a little ritual of taking them all a presentation copy of my latest book—there was usually at least one a year—which they at least had the grace to take away with them, whatever they did with them afterwards—and that is why, you see, I am beginning to consider if there might be a different way to end the tontine.

"Yes, certainly they read my books. Farwood, the moun-taineer, who died in the Andes, had one with him at his base camp: another was by the bedside of Knighton, the plant-hunter—the black poppy man, you know?—when he succumbed to malaria in Burma; even my old friend Vine, the mathematician, had one with him in his last days in a nursing home for the, for the, shall we say, *perplexed*? And all the others too. On each occasion, their heirs were good enough to write to tell me what pleasure their late relations got from my books, and to return their copies to me as a keepsake. I saw then that they had even marked some passages in the margin."

His aged host beamed, and his watery eyes gleamed.

"And there they are." The last mourner gestured towards a bookcase in the corner of the room, in a warm walnut wood, with a fine glazed front. "I shall show you some."

The books were battered and brittle: they certainly showed the signs of much handling. Their author touched them tenderly, as if they were precious relics. To Lorne, used to dealing with books that had a distinguished or unusual provenance, there nevertheless came a certain delicate quiver. These volumes had known the fingers of a most peculiar cenacle of men, eccentrics, explorers, advanced thinkers, adventurers. And it was as if something of their aura still lay upon the fog-coloured paper and the drab card covers. Inside, as Blanch pointed out to him, were the valued signatures of his friends. And he flickered through the coarse-grained leaves to show where bold underlinings and circlings, arrows and vertical slashes had been scored by the book's late owners at particular points in the text.

Then, into Lorne's trained and attentive book cataloguer's mind, there stole a cruel suggestion. He found himself wondering uncharitably if it had been entirely straight-faced pleasure that Blanch's friends had derived from his books. He could imagine them being in the nature of a shared joke between the other survivors, the pulpiest bits marked in ecstatic pencil for comparison later. He looked again quickly at the markings in one or two of the books. The pencilled exclamations seemed to speak to him in a new satirical tongue, as if their grey shades were floating from the page to invest his imagination. And he heard in his head their dark sardonic laughter. He closed the books carefully and helped the old man replace them in their places. The author's lank white hair was flopping over his watchful face as he nodded his head.

"Yes, I do not mind saying I drew a certain succour from the affection these friends had for my work. Not all the reviewers, you see, have been so kind. But do I mind, sir? I do not, when I consider what comfort and ease my books have brought me, and how they have most probably prolonged a life that did not seem at the beginning likely to have such a full measure. So it is that I am left with the last hoard of the Tontine of Thirteen. And there is a delicate choice to be made. Should I conform to the exact letter of our agreement, made so long ago, and conclude arrangements with some glinting-eyed thanatist for twelve empty black carriages to attend my own internment? Well, you have seen: it is not possible. That motley collection of carts was the best I could do. It was a travesty. No, do not demur. I do not want this at my obsequies. Should I instead, as I am sure some would now urge me, put the not inconsiderable money to more mundane charitable use?

"No, no, it will not do. Recently a happy idea has come to me. I have gone into the matter with my legal man, who has said he doubts if our deed ever had any true validity, and (invoking here common sense rather than the law, a distinction he said he was often compelled to draw) asked who was there to mount a costly challenge upon so obscure a matter? So, it is all but settled. Can you guess my idea, young man?"

The old man giggled, with an unpleasant gurgling noise, and his countenance seemed to gleam with the cold pure sheen of alabaster. Lorne shook his head.

"I shall draw upon the fund, while I am yet still living, to pay for the issue of the final work in my series, *The Last of Saprophyte,* which I may tell you confidentially publishers are singularly unwilling to put out, at least without a subvention. I shall assuage my not greatly troubled conscience by including at its head a memorial essay on the twelve friends that have preceded me, and dedicating it to them, who read and relished so many of its ancestors. Yes, I do think that is quite the best solution. Don't you agree?"

Lorne made assenting murmurs as unemphatically as he could, and then made to go. Uchtred Blanch did not try to detain him. At the door he offered his visitor a wan hand. "Do call again, young man, won't you? I am sure I shall have a copy of my last volume ready for you. I can see you would enjoy it."

There was something in the stare that accompanied this remark, and in the intonation of the voice, some slight emphasis on the *you*, that made Lorne wonder if after all Blanch had always known: was perfectly aware of his friends' sporting with his books; and that it was this fierce intelligence that had driven him to outlive them all, and have the last of the laughter.

Morpheus House

The morning post brought to the door of Morpheus House, through the brass letter-box with its crust of verdigris, a cockatrice, a stilt-walker, a corridor made of veils of light, a stuffed humming-bird that spoke, a journey on a train that ran across country (without the use of tracks), an angel from Lemuria, and a quest for a chess seal, whatever that might be.

The curator looked at them all solemnly and considered to which categories they each belonged, writing out a docket for each one, with a cross-reference to the date. Then she placed them into folders according to their date. She placed the dockets in the long narrow oak drawers corresponding to their theme, and she reserved the chronological folders for later arrivals. Really, that was all the work that she must do today, unless there was an afternoon post, which there seldom was; and it had occupied her rather less than an hour.

Yet if it had been suggested to Lorna Tablay that her job was somewhat of a sinecure, she would have gently but firmly demurred. For, there always seemed some other matter to attend to. Sometimes the letters required a reply, sometimes there were cheques or postal orders to handle. Then, once a quarter, there was the journal to compile, no easy matter. Moreover, it was not always obvious which category was apt to use in each case; it was a matter for scrupulous judgement, thinking, not of what the image might mean for her, but of how others might seek for it—even though only a few ever did.

She had a strong face with rather blunt features—a nose, chin and brow that had something plainly monumental about them, as if carved by a journeyman, not a master. But they were relieved by kind hazel-hued eyes which, peering through wide round glasses, always seemed faintly puzzled. Her woody hair, cut short above the neck, sat uneasily upon her, raggedy but with a certain wild symmetry, like a rook's nest.

For most of the days, for most of the weeks, though Morpheus House was open, she was alone in it. Twice a year the trustees met here, five of them, and heard her reports, and praised her, and wondered how best to advance the work of the House, always without conclusion. Rarely, one or two of them might call in, or some other official might have administrative business there, making her really quite busy for a while on some routine matter. And perhaps there might be thirty visitors or so in the year from amongst the Correspondents, who were the mainstay of the house. But she had only three regular callers, and all of them were expected later this day: Mara, the artist who came to share lunch with her once a week; Mr. Jellicoe an elderly man who came to look for "Signs", perhaps also simply for company; and Richard Manifold, a researcher at the university, who was writing a thesis, he said, on "Aspects of the Edwardian Unconscious", whose visits she found welcome but unsettling.

Morpheus House (1903), to give its general title, had been founded, on philanthropic principles, for the purpose of collecting and cross-referencing dreams. Its Edwardian inventors, Sir Edward Cedric Barnaby FRS, Miss Bozeat, Dr. Anand, and Hugh Northcote, had reasoned that virtually all of humankind's attention had been given to its waking life, none at all to what went on while it slept. A studious analysis of the incidents, imagery, and experiences of the dreamer might reveal patterns and implications that would otherwise elude noetic science. It rapidly gathered to itself a circle of

Correspondents who undertook to record whatever they could recall of their dreams. Many of these had made a duty of it all their lives, urging others to do likewise. Their numbers were dwindling now, it was true, but their devotion did not.

The house itself was not grand, indeed it was more like the retirement villa of some prosperous professional man or merchant. Its address was in a modest provincial town and it lay even in the backwaters of that, off a winding lime avenue that led cautiously out to the country. Its outer face was of tawny stone and its only character was in two round windows on the upper floor at either wing. In each of these had been placed an alabaster head, gazing out upon the quiet street: one, with wings at its temples, was said to be of Morpheus; the other, with white closed eyelids, was Hypnos. They seemed to Lorna, whenever she approached the house, to be its guardian spirits: there was something at the same time strange yet comforting about them. If one day she were to look up and fail to see them, she knew it would send a pang of alarm through her: and so they were always the first thing she sought, as she drew near.

On this morning, she had sought for them more keenly than usual. For a white clammy mist had risen in the little town overnight, drawing its cerement veils over walls and trees and rendering them faint and unreal, and subduing the amber streetlamps into feeble aureoles, as if they were so many ranks of diminished angels whose halos no longer shone with righteous fire. Even though she knew so well the way, she had to look out carefully for the house and then peer up quickly to find the round windows and their white guardians.

Once inside, she felt she could shut the door on the chill, paled town and find consolation in the work of the House. Having docketed all the dreams satisfactorily, she made herself a beaker of jasmine tea and reflected on what task to tackle next, watching the steam emanate slowly upwards in graceful veils. The least interesting part of her work was the compilation of the almost algebraic tables which appeared as an appendix to each issue of the journal, a numerical analysis of all the reports received in the previous quarter. In all of the time she had worked here, which must now be nearing ten years, she had never herself observed any really significant patterns in the accounts of dreams she handled, but she was convinced that even if there were something to be discerned, it would not be through these numbers. It must, instead, she thought, be through some intuitive leap of recognition, some creative making of connections between images that might otherwise seem disparate.

To take today's correspondence, for example: when Gerald Fenner reported that he walked a long way down a corridor of wavering, gauzy light, and Lady Lyllian that she piloted a train ("a steam train, you know") across the hills and meadows of some pleasing but unremarkable country, but on no line of any kind, they would both be recorded as experiencing a journey. And Mr. Scribble's (his name always indistinguishable) cockatrice, and Miss Snaith's talking humming bird were both "encounters with curious creatures". Yet it could be that the real, undivined and uncomprehended, link was between the cockatrice and the corridor of light, or the steam train and the humming-bird.

Oddly enough, Lorna herself seldom dreamt at night, or seldom remembered if she did. She warmed her pale palms against the walls of the teacup, yet still felt a little shiver course its way through her, despite the green woollen cardigan she wore over her checked frock. It was true, though, she reminded herself, that she did day-dream quite a lot. Now, day-dreams—the art of reverie, waking, wandering thoughts—were no part of the business of Morpheus House (1903), and never had been. Perhaps the founders had thought them still too close to the conscious mind to warrant investigation. Yet that was a shame, in a way, for she often caught herself exploring curious byways, just as her Correspondents did in their sleeping-dreams: and she supposed others must do the same.

She would find herself wondering, for example, both about her work and about herself. As to the work, she often pondered that too much of the House's time was devoted to the collection of the dreams, and not enough to reflections upon their causes—or consequences, if any. Suppose, she mused, that dreams were just one direction that the mind, or the soul, could take when it settled into sleep; suppose there was another path, hard to see and overgrown, which the sleeper could take, where there was something other than dreams, some unguessable, unrecorded experience. Or suppose people were not so much dreaming, as being dreamt? And, as to herself, she would think about whether anything was going to happen to her that would be different to the days that had passed already. She was not sure that she wanted this: but she was sure that she liked to think about it, and what form some such irruption into her settled days might take. Imagine—the thought would make her smile—that something of the hoard of dreams recorded in the House should suddenly escape, and exert its influence upon her.

But day-dreams would not do. So she finished her drink and went to survey again the neat rows of oak cabinets containing the recorded dreams of so many years: perhaps, she had once worked out, nearly one hundred thousand separate records. She opened one of the long sliding drawers at random and plucked out the fawn-coloured card. It bore the handwriting, with its straight black spikes like the palings of a park fence, of her predecessor.

Lorna Tablay looked at the message inscribed on the card, frowning to decipher the script. Y6t77yhu, it seemed to say. She stared at it harder. The house around her was quite silent.

The glazed and gilt-lined portraits of the founders gazed down upon her, the whorls in the grain of the old polished wood in the cabinets and cases were heightened by a weak light from without, which whispered through the good thick glass of the tall windows; the wall-clock clicked quietly to itself. She tapped the card she had chosen against the thumb and forefinger of her ungarnished left hand, as if she might in this way shake out the meaning of its text. Then she once more gave it her regard, and this time the words formed themselves almost clearly. They seemed to say: "Younger woman's face, staring".

She looked up, and looked about her. The record room remained orderly. Nothing was out of place. It would be just the same if she were not there, if no-one was there. She took the card over to the window which looked out on to the empty avenue. There was a murmured bloom of dim light here and she tilted the card towards it. Its dull hue intensified slightly and the dark writing took more depth upon itself. The message, under this new scrutiny, remained the same: "Younger woman's face, staring". It was dated twenty-seven years ago.

When the trustees had first started their work, she knew, a great deal of attention had been given to the question of whether there were prophetic dreams. That interested people very much, because it opened up so many possibilities. They had flippant enquiries—she had been shown some of them—in the early days from young men who wanted to know if any of their Correspondents could "put them on to a good thing with the gee-gees" or "tip them the wink on the markets". A few striking case studies were encountered—not about horses or stocks and shares—where some inkling of things to be might be made out from the account of a dream. But, certainly more significantly, there were many hundreds more cases where no such omen was given—or, at any rate, not one that could be discerned from the diurnal concerns that came to the dreamer in the days that followed. Perhaps, Correspondents then suggested, the message, if there were one, had simply not been understood—or perhaps it bore significance in some other sphere entirely than this one?

Those debates did not run now. Prophecies and omens were no longer searched for. And nor could a dream like this cast any light upon the subject anyway, for it was too vague. Was *she* a younger woman? Perhaps, just. She ran her fingers through her tangle of hair, and moistened her worm-coloured lips. Then, with a sigh, she carefully replaced the card in its ordained niche, and went upstairs to tidy the meeting room, which did not need it. As she entered, she drew up with a start: opposite, framed in the round window, hovering above the white mask of winged Morpheus, was a face, a hazy, quivering smudge of flesh. Dust motes trickled slowly in front of her as she caught her breath. Then, as she gazed, she realised what it was. Her own face, reflected in the tilt of the window where it caught the weak light coughing through the mist; her own face, nothing more. She made a grimace at herself: and so did the glass simulacrum. She pushed the door further open and made a great to-do of straightening the desk-jotters, checking the stationery. Visits to the other rooms—the small library, the "quiet room" (as if they were not all very quiet indeed), the little kitchen, the trustees' office—were accompanied by equally perfunctory and unnecessary tasks. Then, with something of relief, she heard the rattle of the door and Mara's bright voice hailing her.

Her friend was an artist with no imagination. So they had a very simple, harmless and convenient arrangement. For her part, Mara provided the pen-and-ink illustrations, perhaps four or five every time, that appeared in the quarterly journal: people said they liked them, sometimes enthused how well she had captured the key images of their dreams. In return,

Lorna let her look at the forms and letters received from Correspondents, whose dream-images often gave a sufficient jolt to her art. She would riffle through these papers rapidly, putting some aside; and then she would choose one or two, and think about them with a tightening of her eyes. It was seldom she failed to find "inspiration" in this way.

"Well, what have you got for me? Whoohoo, that mist is hanging about a bit. It bites your bones." Mara threw aside a painted scarf in tinctures of maroon, dropped her yawning velveteen bag, and settled on a sagging chair in the snug, or parlour, that lay to the east of the house, under the protection of Hypnos. Lorna showed her the dated folders. "Diddledy-dum, diddley-dum," said Mara as she sifted through these at some speed.

"Did you ever wonder, darling, if any of your splendid people made these things up?" she suddenly asked. "I mean, just suppose you really want to please that dear girl at the Morph H, and you haven't sent her anything for simply ages; wouldn't you just dash down any old thing? Like, look at this . . . "

She flapped a flimsy form which seemed like a frail creature caught in her bejewelled claws.

" 'I am drifting in a funeral barge on a slow green river. Exotic animals—monkeys, parakeets—line the banks and seem to be mourning me. The boat has no pilot, but knows where it is going. I lie listening to the gibbering, and the gentle rippling.' "

"Journey," said Lorna to herself. "File with the steam train and the tunnel of light."

"Listening to her old man's snoring, and the gurgling of the plumbing, more likely!" And Mara cackled at her own interpretation.

"Still," she continued, "I quite like it. I could stick something stately and golden on the old canal. That'd fetch them.

Surreal it would be. Well, dear, have a sandwich, and some chopped celery."

"Fetching them"—those who paid for her pictures—was a perennial consideration.

They started to eat their lunch in a contented silence.

"If some of them make things up, they aren't very inventive," Lorna remarked, since it seemed as if the silence had gone on long enough. "I pulled out one just at random this morning, and all it said was: 'Younger woman's face, staring.'"

Mara paused in mid-crunch and waved a piece of celery. "Well, that sounds like a real one, you'd hardly bother making that up. I don't even know why they sent it in."

"Oh, it was years ago," said Lorna.

"Eh? But who was it?"

"I didn't look."

"Honestly! You're giving me half the story here . . . "

"Well, I couldn't find it again if I tried. There's just masses of them."

Mara put down her plate. "Tell you what, I'll have a go. Let me just choose a dream. Sounds like a song-title, doesn't it?" And she began extemporising a tune around the phrase, singing "I'll Choose a Dream" in a full, rather throaty descant. She tripped out into the great record room, and Lorna could hear her loud footsteps, almost like the tick-tock of a grand clock, as she wandered among the rows of files.

"Here, this will do." From the parlour, Lorna could hear the oak drawer make its familiar sliding sound, then a pause. It seemed more than usually quiet, in contrast to Mara's boisterousness.

"What does it say?" she called. Mara did not reply at once.

There was a loud cackle. "That'll teach me," her friend called back.

Lorna went to join her. Mara waved the index card.

"It's blank—completely blank."

Lorna looked puzzled. "That shouldn't happen," she said, and took it from her. It was a docket like all the others used to record notes of dreams, but it had not been completed. There was nothing at all on the card. She frowned.

"Not to worry, my deary. I expect it was just used as a filler or marker in some way. Anyway, that's all I get for mucking around!"

They returned to the parlour and finished their lunch. Mara looked again at the recent reports and made a few more notes of things she could paint that other people had dreamt. She packed up her velveteen bag and made her cheery adieus. The house settled back into silence.

ℰↄ

At half past two promptly, as he nearly always was, Mr. Jellicoe arrived, after his visits to the post office, the newsagent, the chapel, and the retired people's club (for lunch). Lorna was expecting him and had kept an eye on the door. As usual, he pushed it open very gently and peered around the edge. "Anyone home?" he called. "Come in, Mr. Jellicoe, do," she replied. He was lean, had silver hair the hue of frosted glass, and green eyes that were just slightly distant. When he spoke to you, it was as if they were always seeing—or looking for—something over your shoulder, beyond. He took off his fawn raincoat and rested his red tartan bag, where a paper and a bible and a flask jostled, on the floor by his chair. He poured them both a lukewarm, mud-coloured coffee from the flask. Lorna offered arrowroot biscuits.

"Well," he said, at last, "any Signs, do you think? The sky was very red this morning, you know, it made the mist seem on fire." He always used the word "Sign" with an audible capital letter. Mr. Jellicoe, for so frail a man, had a very resolute faith in the imminence of the Second Coming and sought everywhere for the Signs of it. He knew the biblical prophecies thoroughly, and it was surprising to Lorna how many different things could be interpreted as a Sign.

"Oh, I couldn't say, I don't have your learning, Mr. Jellicoe," she said, but handed him the folders of recent correspondence. He handled these tentatively, as if not quite sure what he would find or what they might tell him. But there seemed to be nothing there for him. Not the cockatrice, nor the stilt-walker; neither the humming-bird, nor the train journey, seemed to speak of the nearness of the numinous. The angel from Lemuria naturally detained him a little, but as he appeared in the dream in the guise of a bartender mixing cocktails, it was hard to read divine revelation into this vision. His cautious, green-veined fingers let the papers flicker back into place.

Seeing his crestfallen face, Lorna tried to offer consolation. "I thought I'd have a look at some of the earlier dreams, this morning," she said. "And I took one out just out of chance, and do you know what it said? It said 'Younger woman's face, staring'."

He looked at her as if he wanted her to believe he had understood, though he hadn't. "I see."

"And then our artist, for the journal, you know—she tried. And—guess?"

He shook his head, more frank with her this time.

"Just a blank card. Not a thing."

"Not a thing," he repeated. But he was still puzzled. Neither of these were Signs. Why would he want to know about them? He pursed his lips and looked at her politely.

Lorna was finding the conversation a little hard to sustain. So, without meaning to, she said: "Why don't you have a go?"

Enlightenment rose in him. Ah. That was it. He was to "have a go" too.

"Oh, I hardly like . . . " But she looked so eager, he pottered out to the record room and looked, rather bewildered, at the rows and rows of—the phrase came to him unbidden—dead dreams. He reflected. Was it really quite right to just dip in, like that? Wasn't it, well, *sortilège*, which the Book expressly forbade? Could one just, as it were, conjure a Sign up from the past? But though his faith was strong, his sense of courtesy was stronger still, so he felt he must oblige her.

Still hesitantly, he slid open a long oak drawer with tentative care, and reached inside. His fingers hovered, trembling—though from infirmity, not from trepidation. They closed on a card and it came away. He took it back to the parlour where Miss Tablay smiled at him, expectantly. He peered at it, then adjusted his gaze outwards again.

"There is a dream here," he announced, "where there is a house and the walls are made of gravestones, some very old, in antique script, and the person doesn't want to go inside as it seems cold and the light is murky and green." He became thoughtful, then a gleam sparked in his eyes.

"Now at the Last Day, when Israfel blows his horn . . ." (he chuckled a little at that) "we are told of course that the dead will throw back their tombstones and emerge from the grave, all for judgement." He stopped and paused to weigh the prophecy against the dream, or Sign. Something was perhaps lacking, for he sighed and his eyes, like old moss, seemed furred over somewhat. "Well," he said. "Well, well."

"At least it was more interesting than the blank one," ventured Lorna, brightly. He nodded. There was a stillness while he quietly finished his coffee and considered the Sign carefully and whether, being from so long ago, it counted: whether bringing it out again into the light of day, even the dim light of this day, meant that it had become new again, risen with new meaning. It was a difficult consideration. Was it really any better than the blank card, which might signify the end of all? But soon it was time for him to go, and he gathered up his coat and bag, thanked her for her help, and made his way to the door, still bowed in thought. His leaving was as unobtrusive as his arrival, and the silence he left not so very different to the silence he had occupied with her.

ℬ

Richard Manifold, with his pointed, rather Elizabethan beard, dark features and slightly too affected tailoring—a plum waistcoat, a rich red-and-black tie, a country suit of agate-tinted tweed threads, rust coloured socks—arrived in his breezy fashion about an hour later. He put his valise down firmly on a desk and drew out his notes and writing instruments. He had no interest in the recent arrivals amongst the dreams and treated Miss Tablay to a courteous monologue that brooked, however, of no reply or idle talk.

"Good afternoon. May I consult the archives once again? I can quite see to myself, I shall be no trouble. Through here, as usual?"

Lorna nodded and murmured. She heard the oak drawers slide repeatedly open as the young researcher riffled through them. It did not seem gainly to wait around in the next room while he worked, so she went upstairs again and took another look in the meeting room. There was nothing to do there at all, so she walked to the window where the head of Morpheus sent its winged stare beyond. Her face, rippled and wavering, was once again cast back wanly at her in the window. It was growing dark early, there were still gatherings of the dank mist lingering in the lane, and there was little else to be discerned. There was a greyed, dreary whiteness, and that was all. Still, she stared out for a little while, as if the dulled scene was drawing her to its gloom, and found herself succumbing, half-willingly, to another reverie. A passer-by, hunched against the chill air, might peer upwards through the murk and make out the cold white stare of the alabaster head, then dimly see above this another white figure, less defined, hovering insubstantially.

Through her reverie, she thought she heard her visitor calling her name and it seemed as if she wandered slowly down the stairs to see him. In the faltering light, she took each step carefully, so that the stairs seemed to go on longer than usual. When she had descended, Mr. Manifold was propped in a rather studiedly nonchalant fashion against a desk in the entrance hall, as if he were waiting for her.

"I am really quite at a loss," he said. His eyebrows arrowed upwards plaintively. "There is simply far, far too much here. Far too much. I will never understand what was playing around all these old Edwardians' minds, not if I stay here a century. All of my notes—" (he sighed, extravagantly) "are so much chaff. Chaff!"

Miss Tablay tried to look professional and concerned but really his chagrin was too comical. "May I help you to sort them in some way?" she offered.

He looked at her aslant. "Oh, Miss Tablay. That would only half the task. Instead of over a century it would take the two of us fifty years together." They both fell silent as if giving the prospect serious contemplation.

"Well," she ventured, after a while, "what if you were simply to draw out a representative dream or so?"

"How do you mean?"

So she told him of the dreams taken at random, first by her, then by Mara, then by Mr. Jellicoe. He nodded slowly. They both returned to the record room.

He wrenched open a file brusquely. "What about this?" Out came a card: he barely glanced at it. "Or this." Out came another. He seized another drawer. "Or this. Or this." Soon he was taking fistfuls of cards, and then, with a sudden gesture, he flicked them all onto the floor, where they lay sprawled.

"Oh! I say, don't please. I'll only have to tidy them up."

"Really? Really? Who would care, for a dozen dreams less? Who would know? Go on, let them free, throw them out into this ugly old world. Come on, let's see how many dreams we can release."

There seemed to her a curious quickening of the air, as if time had taken a leap or the force of gravity had momentarily been lifted. Suddenly, something of his mad mood caught her up, and she advanced, cautiously at first, towards his side. Then she too started to wrest the dockets from their places. Together they seized them, handful by handful, and, with a whoop of joy, threw them in the air. In the dim, dusty light they spiralled down softly and slowly—dreams of birds, bells and books, spiders, spectacles, and statues, devils, diamonds and dinosaurs, winged men, wolves and windows into other worlds—walls and passages, openings and closures, endings and beginnings, all falling, falling and falling, like the gold dead leaves of autumn, or so much fine and frail dream confetti.

Without Instruments

Here was a plumbing warehouse made of corrugated iron and blackened brick; it had fifteen car-parking bays, none of them occupied. A few clusters of semi-deflated balloons in lurid green and yellow had been attached to drainpipes to give the place a bright air. They succeeded only in making it seem more dismal. It was called "Tap Tap". Alongside this name, in big rounded letters, there was a cartoon of two taps dressed in evening clothes, with metallic feet dancing.

Its neighbour, similar in construction, was called Fairfield Foods. A large oval emblem was blazoned on the building. It showed a golden sun pouring its beams on rounded green meadows on which random fruits had been scattered—strawberries like fresh red wounds, bananas like yellow scythes, grapes like strange black growths. There seemed to be no windows, just fire escape doors painted in bland unsmiling colours, and sealed closely against the walls.

Somewhere about here there was a community hall, the venue for a performance of Ruthven's *Second String Quartet*. It was a work said not to exist, until recently. Perhaps, properly, it still did not exist. Really, it must only be a reconstruction. But, it was claimed, one based on a rediscovered notebook.

Beyond the major names of the musical world there has always existed a twilight of minor figures, known in their time, but soon forgotten. Sometimes they are taken up by enthusiasts, and their work drawn out blinking into the light,

165

briefly resurrected. Often enough this work is done by those interested in local history, keen to connect their own place with anyone remotely eminent: small towns are especially apt to do this.

That was not the case with John Ruthven. He had been born on the edge of a large industrial city that already had enough famous sons and daughters after whom streets, squares, public buildings, and festivals could be named. He might get a few lines in the most diligent guides, but no more. No: Ruthven scholars came from a different community, the wilful admirers of the obscure. There are those who make it a principle not to like anything that is popular, out of a mistrust of mass taste. Those who have never caught on are their preserve. They look with disdain on all the rest.

These obscurantists do not mind too much if they find a few people who share their taste for a shunned figure, provided it is only a few. Even then, however, they are apt to try to outdo each other in the depth of their knowledge of their subject. That was how Farne had come to hear of the performance of Ruthven's supposedly lost work. A correspondent in the informal coterie of the composer's admirers had sent him a carefully offhand e-mail.

Ruthven, by then already fallen into neglect, had in 1963 left his papers to an ancient society of humanists, the Infidels (a name often adopted with pride by unbelievers in the nineteenth century), and died soon after. He had been a lifelong, though largely inactive, member of the Infidels. This institution was itself dying, slowly, and had moved from a quite grand edifice in Southwark to a prefabricated building on the northwestern edges of London, and finally, with its honorary secretary, to a small office in a Staffordshire spa town. During these moves, Ruthven's papers had been consigned to cardboard boxes and sealed up with parcel tape, along with piles of minutes, and out of date brochures.

Not very much was known about Ruthven himself. The few photographs showed a sharp-featured man with rain-coloured eyes, wan hair cut very short, wearing a jacket that seemed blended of the many shades of lichen, a stark white shirt, and a rust-red tie. He lived on the Lincolnshire coast and it was said he seldom welcomed visitors. His exquisite threnody, *Saltfleet*, which people said almost made you taste the sea, was often played, and probably his main source of sustenance; it was what most people remembered him for, if they did at all. The mournful rising and falling chords, repeated with only minor variations, seemed to evoke, almost to become, the eternal restlessness of grey waves on a desolate shore. It was generally assumed that, finding he could not better this work (at least in the ears of the public), he had fallen silent in his last years, issuing nothing new, thought still working.

His papers had been uncovered some years after they were bequeathed, by a particularly persistent admirer, who had found that they included an almost complete score (though with erasures and query marks) of the second string quartet Ruthven had been known to be working on, but had never published. An arranger had been found to put the manuscript in order, making choices at those points where Ruthven had left doubt about his intentions. The final movement of the four ceased in the middle of a phrase; there was a probable trajectory towards an ending, but the discoverer and the arranger had agreed it was better not to do this. Let the phrase, and the work, stay uncompleted.

This was all that Farne had learnt about the work. A moderately competent quartet had been engaged to perform the discovery, and the community hall that had been hired was close to where Ruthven had grown up, though the fields he had known had long been occupied by industrial and commercial buildings. The event was by invitation only, and Farne felt grateful that he had been included.

Julian Farne was forty-five, and alone. He made a living, just about, from buying and selling old postcards. The growth of interest in ancestry and family trees had worked in his favour; people wanted pictures of the places where their forebears had flourished. He also had a more furtive line in Edwardian erotic cards, with their semi-veiled moons of opulent sepia flesh. Sex and the dead always seemed to sell: he supposed it had never been otherwise.

A few years ago, he had discovered a postcard whose view included, in the receding distance, Ruthven's school, long since demolished. No other image of it was known to exist. It was this contribution to Ruthven studies that had established him among the inner circle and, no doubt, led to his invitation.

The pursuit of postcards absorbed him, as well as sustained him. That, and music, the more "on the edge" the better, was what he had. There were acquaintances in both fields. At postcard fairs, he would drink tea out of white plastic cups in the company of a few crusty fellow dealers, and sometimes have a cheese sandwich (as white as the cups) or a cake. They would exchange gossip, listen cautiously to each other, as if not wanting to hear too much. But sometimes Farne would catch himself staring round the hollow, shabby halls where the fairs were held, and wonder what he was doing there. He would look instead at the views on his postcards, with their improbably blue heavens and their soft rolling green hills; why didn't he go there instead? But then, would the view still be the same, seen through his eyes?

He had come to appreciate "difficult" music chiefly as a means of distinguishing himself, in his own eyes as well as in the regard of those few others who took any interest in him. Without it, he feared he would fade into the sort of drab nonentity he saw all too often around him. It pleased him to think that very few knew or understood these works of high modernism.

The journey to the concert venue had been tiresome and, to save money, he had walked from the station. It had taken him half an hour. He felt unfit. He was wearing the nearest his wardrobe could furnish to festive or semi-formal attire: a rubbed black velvet jacket, dusty black shirt, slacks with black and silver humbug stripes, and shiny pointed shoes. It had seemed apt for the concert performance, but, he was conscious, was less so for this slog in uncertain terrain. The last five minutes had involved a haul uphill on the margins of a busy dual carriageway. Where were all these pallid figures going, in their painted boxes? His flesh had become clammy, and his long, lank and faded hair clung to his scalp, and clustered moistly around his neck. He reflected that he was in plenty of time, so he slowed down and began to notice the buildings around him: the plumbing warehouse, the food refinery. What would Ruthven have made of those? "Tap Tap"—surely that sounded like an unwelcome intrusion, the tap on the shoulder we least expect?

On a rusted pole tilted at a slight angle, there was a sign in bleached-out lettering, which could be construed as reading "Community Centre". There had been attempts to make it suggest something blunter. It now pointed midway to the sky. At its base the asphalt was cracked like blackened lips. Farne followed what he thought might have been the original direction. He passed a building with darkened windows which seemed to be owned, or occupied, by a concern called "Valu", but what the value was he could not tell. Another building, festooned with brightly coloured plastic letters, said it offered "Funbags, for all your party needs!!" Farne found that the exclamation marks in particular lowered his spirits further. He trudged on, beyond the weed-bordered yards. Ahead, he could see a low, one-storey building of pale brick, relieved by blotches of white-painted wooden panels, now streaked with green spittle. A long ramp like a giant concrete tongue led up to it. From wide experience of the venues for postcard fairs, he recognised the features of a modern public hall.

A swing door in smoked glass gave onto a lobby occupied only by a flecked mat, which bore the imprint of numerous soiled shoes. An almost identical door off this took him into the entrance hall. A young man with a reluctant beard sat at a wobbly table, taking tickets, and offering a photocopied programme, two loosely folded sheets of thin grey paper like tired skin. Earlier arrivals were standing in the corners of the hall, looking at the programme so that it did not seem they had nothing to do, and so that they did not have to talk to anyone.

He found a niche for himself between a fire extinguisher and a stack of unused tables with dark rubberised feet. From here, he caught the thrust of a few conversations from arrivals:

"I recognised him from his avatar. He was . . . well, you know . . . "

"Yes, we came down on the M665 and then cut across . . . "

"All fields then, of course . . . "

"Yes, but have you heard his *Scherzo for Foghorn*? Oh, you must . . . "

Without any obvious word being spoken, it became unobtrusively apparent that people could take their seats. He quickly settled himself into a grey chair with tubular legs and shiny, but grimy, orange cushions. A lot of the others made a great deal of fuss about doing the same. He could not understand how such a simple matter could generate so much indecision, so much scuttering about.

A thin man with an open-necked shirt and narrow brown trousers took his place before the dais and waited for the audience's restlessness to subside, like an expiry of breath. He looked at them as if he were trying to work out how to escape through their midst, and bolt beyond the smoked doors and down the long slither of ramp. There was no microphone and he spoke quietly, vaguely.

"This is all there is," the man began. Farne looked without thinking about it at the backs of the grey chairs, the dank heads of the audience, the blistered off-white paint of the hall. "This is all there is," the man repeated, and spread his arms. "Enjoy it!"

Or had he said, "This is all there is. Endure it!"? Farne could not be sure.

There was a pause, and then a hesitant smattering of applause. Had he been talking only about the composition, Farne wondered, or something else? The words seemed to express, more or less, the philosophy of the Infidels, so far as he understood it.

With a sudden rush of confidence, the announcer garbled out:

"Ladies and gentlemen, the Mercia Ensemble will now perform the world premiere of John Ruthven's *Second String Quartet*."

Farne settled back into his bright, sticky seat, and tilted his head to one side.

Three young women and an older man dressed in black filed out onto the improvised stage to a slightly more confident murmur of applause. They looked at each other, and then briefly bowed their heads. The hair of the young women fell forward, briefly veiling their faces. Farne thought the ensemble all had something awkward about them as they faced the audience, as if they were more used to the company of their instruments than to people. When they took their places, Farne found himself admiring the long, faintly amber-tinted fingers of the women, and even the more knotted, blue-veined ones of the older man. They seemed to possess a depth of grace and tenderness. There was a brittle hush. Without warning, the fingers began to move.

171

Without instruments. That, Farne had already learnt from discussion groups, was the secret of Ruthven's lost work. He had at first thought it merely a tiresome variation on Cage's silent piece, *4'33"*. But the purpose of that, so far as he could tell, had been to get concert-goers to listen to the sounds of their environment, to put a frame around a portrait of incidental noises, and recognise these might be understood as music too. Ruthven, by contrast, wanted his music to be "heard", but in mime. Only those who followed the movements of the players' hands intently could tell what was being performed. And at first, he found himself trying to translate the deft fluttering of the long fingers into the notes and chords they would be producing. He saw that the bass had plunged into an echoing discord, and this was soon taken up by the others, with a shrill high singing from the viola, like a banshee bewildered in a factory. Then the phrases seemed to follow each other with a stark inevitability, but too quickly for him to grasp them properly. He was able, just, to sense a certain remorseless logic in the movements. In his mind, it was as if the hidden machinery of the world had suddenly been made manifest.

Soon, however, he found that he was no longer following the mimed performance of the music, but instead watching the rapt faces and deft flowing hands of the players. Every eyelid flicker, each slight grimace of the mouth, each sudden tucking of a strand of hair behind the ear, came to seem a delicate and precious moment, itself a form of secret music. The thought came to him that the performers really were hearing the music, in their heads, that their mimicked movements produced for them a mental impression of the sounds the instruments would make, just as if they were really playing them. Perhaps that was in part what Ruthven wanted them to know. And he also found himself wondering how often he, or anyone else, really studied another person for any significant period of time, just simply looked at them.

There was a Warhol installation, he knew, which consisted of films where the camera simply stared at a succession of sitters, who were looking straight ahead into its lens. He had watched it once, in a pod in a gallery. It was disturbing and beautiful. And this experience was similar. As he watched the players, their eyes, defiant, dulled, restless, could hardly be endured; the lips were an intimate pleasure to watch, as they flickered in the slightest of gestures, or tautened tight. Even the nostrils and the temples seemed to have a delicate response to the intense, crystalline, imagined music. He understood that he was watching a work made of the lineaments of the human face, the hands, and the tensed body (more sensed than seen); a work he had never even suspected could exist before. Why had he never been able to see such forms like this before?

At the end of the piece, the performers let their hands lapse into their laps, and faced the audience, impassively. There was a brief pause, and then a faint clapping started, like the release of a sigh. People nodded, and moved about in their seats. The lights flickered on in the main part of the hall, yet their grey glare seemed to diminish it. The performers exited in a single row through a side door, their black clothes a burst of darkness. Farne remained in his seat a while, watching the others making their preparations to leave, murmuring to each other.

Some residue of the performance must have stayed in his mind, because he found that he wanted to watch the departing audience as if they were also performers. Their every small action, in putting on coats, stretching their limbs, lowering their heads to whisper, and stepping haltingly towards the door, then looking back and checking they were taking everything with them, fascinated him, as if they were also enacting a silent composition. He could not imagine what the music could be that would result in this series of

173

gestures, what was the hidden rhythm or the plaintive melody. But he knew that he wanted to hear it over and over. The hall gradually emptied, and he found himself repeating many of the gestures of those who had already left, putting on his jacket, and peering around, as if he were responsible for playing a final reprise. He found this meant that he invested every action with a sort of stateliness, a deliberate care.

As he stepped outside, it was dusk. He turned towards the route back to the station. The great massy warehouses gloomed in the grey haze. They seemed, in the dwindling light, insubstantial, as if they were beginning to fade. It came to him that they were really uttering the vast diminishing chords in a slow, a primevally slow movement of mineral and iron. A wind had risen, and the fascia boards and wire fences creaked and grated. The bold, childish letters of the warehouses were dulled, subdued, and their characters could scarcely be read. Yet he still felt them, with a sharp pang, as in the bright clamour of a flute. The yellow glare of the lamp-posts was a trumpet call; his shadow beneath them responded with the murmur of the cello. Beyond, the noise of the great road rose and fell in drones and surges, like a strange mechanical sea; he almost thought he heard the great remorseless ebbing and flowing of Ruthven's signature piece, *Saltfleet*, in the traffic. He walked towards the sound with a measured step, as if he were still a living composition, and every pace a phrase of music.

Four Haunted Figures

Fire Companions

"How did your people come to be here, Abell—you don't go back a long way?"

The young man, Faraday, putting the question gestured languidly towards the outside.

"Oh no. We are still quite the strangers here. We go back, I suppose, only so far as the early seventeen hundreds or so. Before that we were in town, I believe."

"Whatever induced them to come out here?"

This time Mr. Faraday evidently found even a flicker of his hand too much effort, and inclined his head very gently instead, barely disturbing the fair intricate filigree of his hair.

His companion considered the matter for a few moments.

"Ah, well, there is a sort of family tradition about that. It seems my great-great-grand something-or-other uncle acquired a vast fondness for the fen country. He relished the damp air and all of the blessed everlasting water. He was a physician, you know, and apparently had theories . . . "

"Theories?"

"Crackpot ideas, if you like. Most quacks advise against the air here. But with him, I gather, it was just the reverse. He revelled in it, all the fenland ooze you know. Probably just to be contrary. There is a streak of that in our line. You might find it hard to believe."

A cushion, sewn in blackwork, with many convolute interlacings, caught Mr. Abell softly full square in the face, and for a moment seemed almost to wrap itself around him, half-stifling his laughter. He belatedly took a firm hold of a glass of dark thick liquid precariously lodged on the arm of the chair where he lolled.

"Mind out," he cried. "You nearly upset my porter . . . " And, as if to mitigate any further assaults, he at once took a long draught of it, before resuming.

"The old doctor did well out of it, anyway. He bought up the Hall, lived to a ripe old age, even if his wits wandered a bit in the end, and most of all he passed on his wealth to the honourable dynasty whose finest scion you see before you now . . . " Mr. Abell held up a hand in remonstrance as another cushion appeared to be about to be projected toward him.

"Anyway," he said, placatingly, "it's very jolly that you managed to land this berth so close at hand. You've got it quite cosy, I see, but if there's anything you need, I'll have it sent across."

Mr. Faraday yawned, and his slender form, consumed in a scarlet dressing gown (for it was only a little after noon), slowly wriggled to the perpendicular, like an earthworm raising its head reluctantly out of the warm earth. Then, with surprising industry, he gave the thick larch log on the fire a vigorous kick, turning the somnolent grey-scaled creature into a roaring red beast. His pale features took on an uncanny glow—the eye sockets, fine nostrils, cheek hollows were like caverns of rose fire. Having surveyed the effect of his efforts, he put on a cricket glove which had been crouching on the hearth with its white fingers splayed, and rapidly moved the sullen coals cowering in the grate so that they were plunged into the rising flames from the enlivened log.

His friend laughed. "I can think of something you need, anyhow. I'll have a scout around back at the Hall, and see if I can bring a set across tomorrow."

Mr. Abell was as good as his word. When he returned to his friend's marshland cottage, a tall brick structure of plain proportions and a steep slate roof, at the early hour of ten the next morning, he bore with him a large leather cricket bag. He was surprised to find Faraday awake, dressed, breakfasted, and almost spruce.

"Whatever's got over you? I was just going to drop this quietly off."

"You forget I am now gainfully employed. I have hours to keep."

"Hmph! All stuff. As long as you sort out the old heretic's papers and knock off some sort of life and works, you can choose your own time."

"Well, there's a hell of a lot to go at. I thought I'd better make a start. Anyway, I won't have much time for the game, though it was a kind thought."

"What? No, you silly dupe. I just used the cricket bag to bring them over. Convenient size and all that. Have a look . . . "

Mr. Abell undid the bag and turned it over with a flourish, tipping onto the stone floor with a high clangour a tangle of implements. His friend passed his frail snowdrop of a hand over his brow, sighed deeply, and then knelt to examine them. They were all of bronze, quite nicely worked. He examined in turn a poker, with a round knob that gave off a sullen gleam, and a twisted stem; a pair of tongs whose arms ended in outstretched claws; a fork with three delicate tines like the long flicking tongues of serpents; and a shovel, with a blackened blade and a knot at the head of its handle.

"Just what you need. Stick them on the hearth."

"Won't you need them at the Hall?"

"No. Got another set. Found these after hunting about in the cellars a bit."

"They're very decently made. I wonder why they weren't used?"

His friend shrugged. "Fashions you know. The other lot are very artsy-craftsy, you see. Tortured tulips, wafting lilies, that kind of thing. These a bit more in the late baroque mode. Not the thing these days, I gather. I shouldn't wonder if they don't stretch back to the ancient doctor himself."

"Well preserved, though."

"Stout stuff, bronze. And someone had taken good care of them. They were all nicely cocooned in some sort of soft white cloak. Shrouded, you might say."

"I see. Well, thanks very much. It'll certainly save my slippers and gloves."

"Yes. 'S'what I thought. I'll be cutting along. Shall I pop in this p.m. when you've knocked off your studies?"

The fire companions showed signs of use when Mr. Abell returned to his friend's niche later that day; and Faraday was poring over several piles of papers. He looked up when his companion arrived, but did not rise, and gestured towards a cupboard in the cool of the corner where a few dark bottles loomed. Abell helped himself.

"How does it go?"

"Well, I've made a start. Did they know much about him at the Hall at all?"

His friend sipped the black ale.

"My folks? Old 'Freethought' Wilson? Hmm, they knew *of* him. Of course, we didn't mix. Fellow was a Radical and a heathen, you know. But he wasn't called 'Freethought' locally. Everyone knew him as 'Snuffer' Wilson."

"Yes, I heard that: 'For I shall take a mightly candle-snuffer to your fool inferno, and put out its fires forever.' He wrote like a hellfire preacher himself even though he hated all that. He was bitter about the way the thought of damnation frightened the poor and ignorant."

"Not just the ignorant neither. You are getting on with him, I see. Anyhow, I can tell you that around here he was tolerated all right. Fenland tradition. Keep to yourself, say nothing and never mind anybody else's business. Also, I reckon there was a sort of pride in him after a while."

"Yes?"

"Mmm. Oh yes. Of course it was all his heathen friends that got up the oof to buy this place and turn it into a sort of museum. But I happen to know quite a few of the locals stumped up too. They had a kind of respect for him. Ironic, really. He was such a thoroughgoing freethinker, but they treated him like an old country wizard."

"Really?"

"Mind you, his appearance helped: wild white hair and whiskers, hawk's nose, eyes as bright as dandelions. Ha! Anyway, thanks to all that interest in him, it got you this berth—archivist, curator, whatnot."

It had, in fact, been Mr. Abell's squirely influence that had helped preserve Wilson's Cottage, and help manoeuvre his less well-off old college friend into the appointment—but this he would not for worlds have ever mentioned.

After Abell had left him, his friend tried to settle once more to a preliminary sifting of the papers. A green dusk flowed around the isolated cottage, as if the dank waters were releasing their vapours to douse the last of the sun. The country seemed to take on a veil of decay, and the clouds were wraiths of verdigris. Inside, the young scholar felt the change in the air, sighed and put aside for a moment the papers he was studying.

He had made a start on a checklist of "Freethought" (or "Snuffer") Wilson's works, which were many. The man had been a conscientious pamphleteer, often at his own expense. And it seemed that any response to his works resulted in a sardonic fusillade in reply. Some of them were quite amusing, intentionally or otherwise. Wilson had published *An Atlas of Hell, Being a True Guide to the Fiery Regions*, got up to look like a big map book. The scarlet covers depicted a black devil with a pointed beard, horns, and forked tail, wielding the conventional pitchfork, and a flaming torch in its other claw, for good measure. Every page of the book was blank.

But such silent eloquence was far from his usual practice, and Wilson's weakness was to be over-literal, or to assume that his opponents were. One treatise, *The Uttermost Pit*, demonstrated with considerable geological learning that there could not be space within the mineral bowels of the Earth for any chambers big enough to contain all the damned souls of the ages. A third, *Going to Gehenna*, purported to show that the biblical references to the infernal domain were in point of fact to real places of sinister repute, and not to anywhere metaphysical. Wilson lost no opportunity to argue, with any evidence he found to hand, that there could not be any hell or Hades, and so none should fear them.

Faraday put the little thin grey booklets down. He felt the chill of the green miasma outside steal over him, even through the thick walls of his sanctuary. He rose, and studied the smouldering fire in the black iron grate. He was about to apply an encouraging kick to the slumbering log, when his foot in its Turkish slipper paused, and he remembered his friend's gift. The companion set had been thrown unceremoniously into the reedwork basket by the hearth, which held a few crusted logs and kindling sticks.

"Might as well make use of them, I suppose," he murmured to himself, even while he was also regretful of the opportunity to vent his suppressed energies on the unsuspecting log.

He took up the bronze poker by its middle and glanced momentarily at the handsome, glinting orb at its head. Then he put his palm around this, finding it rather warm to the touch, perhaps from the glow of the fire playing upon it, and plied the poker's tip with vigour to the log's carapace, provoking fiery sparks. For good measure, he also rather randomly stirred up the coals. A few red or golden tongues started up. Gratified by his efforts, he propped the poker with more decorum against the stone fireplace, and took up next the tongs, with their little curved claws. These he used to move some of the coals around, where they might catch the flames better. Then he placed the tongs next to the poker. The extra warmth emanating from the fire stole over him, proving his efforts had been worthwhile, and he sighed contentedly. After some moments indulging in the crackling glow, he sank back into his armchair, and gathered up the papers once more.

It might have been an hour or two later when Mr. Faraday's studies, admingled with certain drowsy episodes of gentle slumbering, were broken by a loud clang. His head jerked up, and his fingers clutched at the papers and pamphlets spread about him. For a few startled moments he could not place the echoes ringing in his ears, and cast quick glances around the room. Then he saw that the round-headed poker he had propped up had toppled over, and must have clattered on the sooted hearth-stone.

"Damned thing!" he muttered, with some heat. "Well you can just lie there for now, you little beast. Unless you fancy putting yourself back . . . "

As if in answer to his invitation, the poker gave one final roll towards him, causing a sudden blaze of panic to rise up in him, until he recovered his composure once more.

"Just settling down, I suppose. There *is* a slight slope on that slab."

The poker did not respond further to these observations, and Mr. Faraday returned to his labours. The room was lit only by two small lamps and by the flickering light of the fire, whose shadows played upon the white walls, and soon he found it hard to concentrate on Wilson's vehement treatises. He ceased making notes and began idly flicking through the various monographs and manuscripts scattered around him. His thoughts became more and more abstracted and his gaze was drawn to the glowing cavern of the fireplace. Whether Wilson was right to deny all divinity and all after-life, Mr. Faraday, though a quite modern young man, sincerely doubted; but at any rate, he thought, one could easily see why some of the old heathens worshipped fire: how quickly the mind found shapes in the flames.

Those two smoky forms there, for example, were for all the world like . . . he sat up to stare at them more closely. He was no longer drowsy, all his consciousness was quickened, all his attention fixed hard upon the figures he thought he saw, which seemed to grow in body and definition. They were like two dark manikins, black as silhouettes, and they seemed to cavort in the heart of the fire. One was a huddled, long-gowned, round-capped figure, as if some ancient prepared for bed; the other seemed to be a thing mainly of spikes and scales. As the tongues of fire crackled and danced, this barbed creature seemed always to be lunging at the frocked shape, which writhed and recoiled in response.

The young scholar stared in fascinated dread at the black drama playing out before him, hardly daring to tear his gaze away; yet he seemed to sense from the corner of his vision that the shadows he saw danced on the pale walls too, so that the tableau encompassed the whole room. At last, he felt that he could watch no more of the strange gavotte between the nightgowned figure and the other thing, and with a great effort of the will, he leapt up from his chair, upsetting all the books and papers. He took hold of the first instrument to hand, and drove the shovel hard into the belly of the fire, disturbing all the coals. It was to no avail—the figures burst up again from the pyre. Then he seized unthinkingly at the next component from the set of fire companions, which chanced to be the fork, meant to be used merely for the quaint pleasure of toasting. This he used to pierce the flames and wave at the figures, but it merely had the effect of making them leap higher.

This useless gesture gave him pause, and, collecting himself, he took up with a fine deliberation the tongs, with their little yearning claws, and swiftly took hold of numbers of the coals, to pile them upon the place where the manikins performed. For a few moments, with a hissing sound, the flames were quenched, and Faraday could hear nothing except his own quick breath. And then spurts of scarlet fire thrust upwards once more through fissures in the coals, and still within their cruel red glow danced the two black figures. Faraday found himself, with a surge of baffled anger, in the foolish game of trying to seize hold of one of them with the taloned pincers of the tongs, but it was as if the figures knew what he was about, and they seemed to lunge away from his every thrust. He flung the instrument down in frustration. It was almost as if the sole purpose of each of the fire companions was to goad the writhing forms further, to add to the excitation of the scaly figure and the torments of the gowned shadow.

But he was not quite yet done. With a sort of morbid despair, his sight heated by the glare of the fire, he grasped half-blindly for the poker, which seemed to leap willingly into his hand, and he aimed its tip into the heart of the fire like a brave St. George, and followed through with repeated savage thrusts. But this fiery beast was not for slaying so soon, and all he achieved was to raise the flames higher and higher, and to cause the black figures to rise up with them, still in their dance of lunging and recoiling, so that they seemed to fill all of the cavern of the grate, and to loom in ever more giant shadows upon the walls and the ceiling of the room. Mr. Faraday sank back in frank despair, and the intense heat swept over him. The poker left his grasp and clattered upon the hearth, like a peal of laughing brazen bells. He felt a faintness take possession of him, together with a babble of voices in his head. But, before he succumbed entirely, he clutched at the papers he had been working on, causing them to fall further forward. The great mock map book tumbled and yawned open, and its white pages flapped, offering a brief refreshing fan of cool air to his brow, and even seeming for a flicker of an instant to quieten the flames.

When Mr. Faraday came to, he did not know exactly how long later, the fire had been dimmed to a sullen murmuring, and no shadows danced above it. He raised himself to his knees, passed a pale hand over his brow, which was beaded with cold drops, and began to dust himself off. He saw that the brazen globe at the poker's head lay adrift of its twisted stalk, and there was scattered from it a fall of ashes, brittle and black for the most part, but with some shreds that still showed scorched corners of darkened white, like burned pages. He lifted up the round knob with a careful curiosity, and saw that it was hollow inside, and there were marks around its rim that he could not quite make out. Then, with great delicacy and hesitation, he picked up a few of the fragments that had not been fully blackened. In the dim dull glow of the low fire and the subdued lamplight, he thought he could discern upon them a few characters, written in a dark hand. There was the hint of a flourish that might be the end of a signature, there were deeply incised numerals that might belong to a sequence of clauses, and there were also some curious symbols of no alphabet that he knew, who was learned in Hebrew and Greek; stark, lunging sigils, like little black flames. To his pale fingers, the burnt paper still seemed faintly warm to the touch, and with an impulse Mr. Faraday let the fragments fall from his fingers, to curl with their blackened cousins upon the cold stone slabs.

Then he began slowly to gather together the disturbed books and papers, and, as he reached to close the great blank pages of Wilson's sardonic atlas, a momentary remembrance passed over him, and he shivered, and fretted his brow.

It was some time before any matter towards a possible elucidation of Mr. Faraday's vision came to him. He was a conscientious young man, and resolutely refused to desert the post he had taken up, despite his ordeal; but it must be confessed that his work on Wilson's papers became for a while a little desultory, and there would be times when his friend the squire found him staring at the fire or at the bare walls, or leafing through a big book of blank pages.

But, as he slowly resumed his catalogue and checklist of his subject's voluminous works, he came upon another of the virulent broadsides against belief in an infernal afterlife. In this, the old freethinker described cases he had encountered of those who had been, so he averred, unreasonably oppressed by a sense of sin and its penalties, such that they had indeed made for themselves a torment of this world, whatever it was that awaited them in the next, through overmuch wringing of their spirit; to this treatise, Wilson had given the title of *Hell on Earth* (the only place he would ever admit it existed, and then through the hands or minds of man alone). The scholar dutifully studied the contents, noting the polemicist's examples of poets, hermits, dreamers, gentlewomen, journal-keepers, children and others whose lives had been darkened by anguish at the thought of the torments to come. And then there came a passage which made him start, and stare at the pages hard.

"In case it should be argued that my many instances are all drawn from others' pages, or tales twice removed, I will not forget to mention," wrote Wilson, "a case I heard about almost upon my own doorstep, which the common talk made all too plain to me. It is a striking example of a man of science, skilled in the arts of medicine, a humane and worthy gentleman, a Dr. A—, whose life was yet blighted by the affliction I have repeatedly here described. Even to this day, this good man's great repute in healing and succouring the people of the parish, high and low, sometimes even without fee, is well preserved. He had come to this remote place from a fashionable and prosperous practice in the little arcadia of Islington, not far from London. There were rumours, naturally, of some tragedy, or mystery, that had driven him here, as if good men only act upon such stimulus. But he did not, at any rate, stint our remote corner of his medical skills, and all remarked how deftly he worked, almost as if, it was said, the instruments and potions of his profession flew to his fingers at his command. Yet this high calling and the very great esteem of his neighbours, whether gentle or yeoman, did not bring this Dr. A— the contentment he certainly merited. Always, from the moment of his arrival, he had a little eccentricity in a morbid fear of fire, so that he would suffer them to be lit only in the very coldest of days, and then only muffled up by guards and screens which quite obscured the flames, so they were scarcely to be seen or felt. This might have passed as merely a little oddity, like that (in a later age) of the great satirist Peacock's Mr. Firedamp, who also abhorred all fiery manifestations. But, as he grew in age, this foible in our Dr. A— fostered itself further, and perhaps revealed its true fount, in a vast and overmastering dread of hellfire. On this subject, I learnt, he would often engage the local church raven [this was Mr. Wilson's habitual term for a parson], apparently quite to exhaustion; and it need hardly be said, got little solace there. It was useless, it seems, for this prelate to remind Dr. A— of the many good works to his name, showing that the consolations of the church are all as naught compared to the baseless terrors it engenders. Even when he was reminded of all the healing and comfort his hands had wrought, he would merely say that this was not all his hands had done, though none could ever get any better sense of what he meant.

"This morbid fear soon enough impaired Dr. A—'s mind and he would often be found wandering the furthest reaches of the fenland, looking, so local lore maintains, for a hole he had heard of that was said to be a bottomless well, whose water was never known to dry up, even in the hottest seasons. Thus, we see one more instance among many of a decent man driven awry by the useless fear of perdition, that dark lie still preached today by the purple serpents [by this term Mr. Wilson evidently intended to be meant the bishops] who . . . "—well, and a great deal more, but not to our purpose.

The Antioch Imperial

The sea had long since fled, leaving a region that was neither land nor water, but a stark, flat, almost houseless terrain that had the worst of both, where the earth was dank and heavy and the streams and pools were black and brackish. But here, where the saltmarshes ended, was a relic of the days of prosperity, when ships had once teemed in the little harbour. It was a narrow, cold church, now little-used, and visited only because it was said that perhaps here the faith first came to Britain. Some holy vessel had found a haven on its shore one storm-wracked night, bearing missionaries in the very earliest days, perhaps even the Arimathean sage himself. There were those who, from respect for this legend, still tended to the church that now had no worshippers otherwise; so that a few times a year candle-light shone from its mullioned windows and its single, rusted bell could be heard to give tongue, dolefully tolling from its tower over the desolate marshes and the wide, untroubled crust of sand. The congregation on these occasions was few, and those mostly the myth-keepers, with a handful of dutiful attenders from the remote farms and granges at the edge of the marsh.

The celebrant at Michaelmas was the Revered Mr. Edgar Summer, who held a living in the nearest town, and he was joined by his old college friend Edward Aldgate MA, who (having moderate independent means) was an assiduous traveller, an amateur of many things, including folk-lore, and was attracted, in addition to the opportunity of staying with his friend, by the whiff of the legend he had heard. It must freely be confessed that he did not attend unduly to the progress of the service nor to the appearance of his fellow participants in the rite, but sat in a contented, contemplative fog of thought, wishing only that the church were a little warmer. Indeed, when, part-way through, a late arrival pushed open the great oak door, and the wind seemed to rise up to join them, he noticed with a distinct shiver how the cold crept in, and did not seem to leave again.

At a certain moment, a velvet offertory bag was proffered to him on a long stalk, and he placed some dutiful donation into its gaping maw. The sidesman continued his way down the aisle until all had been invited to contribute their mite. The last clank of a coin dropping into the bag was followed by a most audible, heavy sigh, almost a wail, which merged with the high wind outside, and Mr. Aldgate reflected that someone was indeed reluctant to part with their treasure. He turned as inconspicuously as he could, and saw that at the final bench, on its very edge, as if the occupant were not sure of their place and wanted to be ready to leave in haste, there was a young man with a grave face. He was swathed in dark cloaks—small wonder, given how bitter it must be outside—and these accentuated the pallor of what little of his flesh could be seen: his long white fingers and the sharp, salt-white temples and brow. In contrast, his hooded hair seemed riotously golden, and there came into Aldgate's mind the absurd idea that it was like a disarranged halo.

Upon the conclusion of the service, he waited with his friend at the door, where (as was the custom) the vicar shook the hand of each of those who had attended the service, who filed out in order from the front pew onwards. Here was old Sir George Trevethick, with his white mane of hair, said to be the descendant of the last man to leave Lyonesse before it was drowned, and an adherent of the Arimathean legend. He was followed by staunch Mrs. Whitgift, a generous benefactor in a purple tweed suit, her ruddy face topped by a pudding basin haircut, who pumped the parson's hand with vigour, and Aldgate's too for good measure. Then there followed a dozen or so others, votaries of the cult of the holy visitors, or local country people, until the last to leave, the gaunt, golden-curled young man, who stared at them as if he would ask something, but he kept his silence and did not offer his hand. Aldgate was glad there were no more, for here the high, keen wind rose up again and assailed them where they stood, looking out from the doorway to the dismal saltmarsh plain beyond and the single narrow track that crossed its drear expanse. The last figure made his huddled way along this, and the two watched him pace, with weariness it seemed, the long straight track, until his body seemed to merge with the grey of the wintry horizon.

Since there was no warden or clerk for the all-but-disused church, the presiding minister took the collection away with him and, since its yield was invariably modest, also counted the money himself before adding it to a fund for the upkeep of the lonely sanctuary. As the way back was tedious, and bleak, the Revd. Mr. Summer had made himself as comfortable as possible in the small, scarcely-used sexton's cottage that lay in the lee of the church. Here the two friends made the best of it with a hamper of viands they had brought along, got a sort of fire going and for a while fortified themselves while they watched the blue flames of the bleached, salted wood. Afterwards, over a pipe with his scholarly friend, the parson mechanically divided the collection into quantities of a shilling and then a pound, without giving them very much attention as he conversed amiably of the old days with Mr. Aldgate. And then his fingers seemed to pause of their own accord, for the shining silver disc they had encountered belonged to none of the coins of the realm. He looked down, took up the unfamiliar piece, and frowned. It was, alas, not uncommon for churchgoers to place in the offering coins for which they had no use: trade tokens, out-of-date money, foreign currency. Yet this was surely out of the ordinary run of those mischievous things. It was heavy and worn and had about it an aura of the ancient. And as he turned it in his grip, he thought that it was unusually cold; there was a brittle chill to it which made itself felt even through fingers scorched by the warmth of the pipe-bowl.

"What do you make of that?" he asked, passing the coin to his friend. The latter did not look at it straightaway, but continued with the cricketing anecdote he had been relating—"and then the raven dropped the bail at long leg"—until something, Summer perceived, in the feel of the coin he had just been passed made him pause, and he glanced down at it. Then he looked at it harder, and held it up to the light of the oil lamp, turning it over to consider both sides.

"This was in the offertory bag?" he asked, and there was a thickness in his voice. "Well, that is curious."

"Oh? What is it?" The clergyman knew that his friend had made a special study of ancient numismatics, and had certain theories of his own. He so far enjoyed his company, that he did not mind provoking one of these.

"It is a Greek Imperial stater of Antioch, almost two thousand years old. You see it bears the head of Augustus, facing to the east and crowned with laurels, and there is this fine beading around the circumference. And on the reverse we have the 'genius' of Antioch, the city's tutelary spirit, draped, and with a turreted crown, holding in her right hand a palm branch; below her, the sea-god Orontes rising from the waves."

"You have seen one before?"

"Certainly, several times. At an ancient ruined Armenian cathedral; in the care of a race who claim to be descendants of the crusaders, who fled to the fastnesses of Georgia; in a palace museum at Trebizond, which kept treasures rescued from the plundered relics of the Byzantine Emperors following the fall of Constantinople; and one which was said to come from a citadel which was the last stronghold of the Assyrians before they succumbed to the crescent."

"You seem to have remembered those quite clearly."

"Yes, well I might."

"Oh? How so?"

Mr. Aldgate was thoughtful. He nodded slowly to himself, and his delicate eyelashes ruffled their wings over his pale eyes in their sunken sockets.

"I will tell you why, but I quite expect you to jib at what I shall say. Have you ever considered what exactly were the silver coins given to Judas? I have given the matter a great deal of careful deliberation. There are passages, as you know, in Zechariah and Exodus which also allude to thirty pieces of silver, and here they evidently refer to the large coins known as shekels. But there were no such coins current in the time of Christ. Probably, therefore, the author of the book of Matthew had in mind a Greek coin quite similar: the tetradrachm or silver stater. Such coins would have been in circulation among the people of Jerusalem, mostly from the Hellene cities, with Antioch perhaps the greatest of these, whose issues were most prevalent. Some such coin as this would have been what Judas was given."

"That is most interesting. You were ever deep in your delvings when a thing took your fancy, Aldgate. So those places you mentioned—they each have a specimen from the period too?"

"No, Summer, not a specimen. They say they have a cursed relic, one of the actual coins."

The parson was a broad-minded man, never willing to mock at the beliefs of others, but it was all he could do to contain a snort.

"The very idea. Rather too like all those pieces of the True Cross in the Middle Ages, enough to build a boat, they say."

Aldgate did not reply. "How very cold the coin is," he murmured. "I cannot seem to warm it, even between my palms."

The cleric decided it was time to dismiss the matter.

"Well, it was a very odd thing to put in my collection, I must say. An old golden sovereign would have been much more welcome. Still—" (he recovered himself hastily) "—each must give what they can, of course. Perhaps one of the farm workers found it while out digging in the fields."

But he knew that he hardly sounded convinced by this homely hypothesis. And then, despite himself, he felt his curiosity still stirred.

"How did those other places get hold of theirs, by the way?"

His friend put the coin down upon the scarred old table where they had spread their food, and reflected. When he had been out on his grand tour of the East, it had been no small matter to secure consent to scrutinise the relics they held, still more to elicit the story told about them. But often they were stewarded by poor men, haggard relics of what had been; the feeble-minded remains of noble lineages; the lean, forgotten residues of semi-abandoned monasteries; the gap-toothed caretakers of decrepit ruins. A modest honorarium, the flaunting of orders and credentials, even a little gentle deceit, had been deployed when it was necessary; and Mr. Aldgate had not shrunk from these for the sake of his researches. But he was a conscientious man, and so he sighed over those peccadilloes.

"Let us light up another pipe, and I will tell you."

They each set about the business of getting their pipes properly lit and drawing well, and it seemed that both welcomed the opportunity for a thoughtful pause. Then the scholar hesitantly resumed the conversation.

"The fact is, Summer, that they all tell pretty much the same tale. Of course, that is quite often the case with legendary lore, but these were places far apart in distance and, I might almost say, in time. The sum of it is that a stranger came to them seeking shelter, lean and golden-haired, and accepted what little they could offer without complaint. Then when he left, without a farewell to any, it was found that some such coin as this had been placed in their alms box."

"I see. Pretty much how that one came to us, then. Anything else?"

"Those are the bare outlines. The rest is the smithwork they forge around them. What outlander, they say, seemingly a perennial wanderer, would come looking for refuge, as if he were destitute, and then leave a silver coin behind? Why does he always choose the very most ancient and sacred places? Who else could it be but the great betrayer, condemned to spend his reward for ever on the face of the earth, and always seeking, yet never finding, a final sanctuary?"

His priestly friend sighed, and then was silent. Beyond the bare cottage, the high wind still wailed. As the salt fire leapt, each man listened intently, though they could not say what they expected to hear: and their inner gaze strayed along the desolate old sea road, where perhaps still strode the strange visitor to that evening's service.

Yogh

"I really don't know what all the fuss is about," said Breckland, of the Oriental School, repining at the way his students had struggled with some aspect of his subject; "It's as simple as A, B, . . ."

We had agreed to try not to talk shop. But Breckland had not quite shaken off the thought of some of the futilities offered up to him at the end of term, and was still apt to fulminate, when at intervals these returned to memory. I admit I was only half-listening. But there was a stir in the corner, and young Maldon, the third of our party, spoke up, something he rarely did. He was usually one of life's listeners, with a gentle, abstracted expression that suggested a certain sympathy with one, whatever his private views might be.

"Well, I'm sure you'll get them to understand it all quite well in the end. But, you know, A, B, C isn't as simple as we sometimes think. Or at least the continuation of it isn't."

Then he lapsed into silence. I went to the window. It was raining steadily. Our idea of tramping over to the remains of the Roman villa at Wherncote would have to be abandoned. It was the fourth day of our stay together: we'd got some good walking in so far, and it wouldn't harm if we loafed for a bit longer here in the parlour we'd reserved for ourselves. Against the grey of the day, the hearth fire blazed pleasingly.

I turned to the other two.

"It's quite set in, you know. I don't fancy getting drenched. So come on, give us the rest of the tale . . . " I cajoled. Then

I started to fill my pipe, as a sure signal that I, at any rate, was quite content not to go out just yet.

Maldon drew his chair closer to the fire.

"It isn't much of a tale, really . . . "

"I was not long on the Faculty, and had been given rooms. They were in quite good order and had a fair view over the college meadows. I enjoyed seeing the trees on the fringes change from bareness to leaf to blossom to fall, as the year went on. I couldn't understand why I, who was quite junior, had been given such spacious rooms, with such a fine prospect, while other, older men had dingier sets. Some of them preferred a gloomy sort of den, of course, but not all.

"And then, after I had been there just a week or two, the little whispering sound began. It was just a—well, a sharp sigh. Nothing more. When there was no-one there. I wouldn't say it worried me, exactly, at first, but I suppose I was always slightly on edge, waiting for the next time I would hear it."

Maldon ran his fingers through a flick of his pale hair.

"Of course, I thought about all the obvious things. The radiators in the place were antiquated and sometimes gurgled like a sea-creature shifting in the sands, but they never sighed. And anyway, the little hiss of breath I heard wasn't always near them. It could be anywhere in my rooms. It also wasn't the wind at the window frames, because I heard it even on balmy days when the trees were still as statues. And it wasn't my neighbours: the walls were quite stout, and the sighs came when no-one was about.

"I didn't at first say anything to anyone else—I didn't want to be thought the nervy sort. But sometimes I noticed a visitor look up sharply, or suddenly stop and listen carefully, so I guessed they had heard something too. That was reassuring, in a way.

200

"However, I also noticed that I heard the sighs more often when I was working at my desk. Sometimes I tried to think it was just the rustle of my papers, but I knew it wasn't . . . "

"What were you working on then?" I asked.

"Early English handwriting. I was aiming to show its development, and also note some regional differences I'd observed."

I nodded.

Breckland also had a question.

"These sighs—were they melancholy, exasperated, or what?"

He was often a master of the exasperated sigh himself.

Maldon paused a bit, in thought.

"That was hard to say. I didn't get a sense of great distress, or frustration. In a way, they were more like a whisper. But without any words, you see? Just a release of breath . . . So, you picture me, working hard . . . "

There was a snort from Breckland.

" . . . working hard, under the lamp, trying to decipher the scrawl of some scribe or clerk, and then hearing, just in the background, that sudden sharp release of breath. I'd put my pen down, stop, look about me, and listen more carefully. But for a while I never saw or heard anything else, until the next sigh came along. I did, however, get a sense of watchfulness. I can't really describe it any other way. There was a sort of intentness in the air. Partly, no doubt, my own extra edge. But not just that. It was as if there was an *expectation* lurking close by me. However, I could not make any more sense of it than that, so, usually, after a little while of waiting, I would just resume my work. The sighs didn't happen often enough to really unsettle me, and I suppose at the back of my mind I imagined there was some kind of explanation in the acoustics of the place, while at the same time not really quite believing that. And then things took another turn.

"I was lying in bed, turning over in my mind some tricky elements in the orthography I was then studying—there were parts hard to make out—when I became aware of a stirring in the darkness. I knew I'd locked and bolted my outer door, and the door to the chamber itself, I always did—I had quite rare and valuable documents in my care, after all. And even the famous nightclimbers, those young men who shinned up drainpipes and roamed over roofs for a dare, were unlikely to get into my rooms, which were of no great interesting height or prominence. So I was quite sure there was nobody else in the room. And yet, there was a definite coiling in the darkness.

"And then, something began to form rather like a black snake. It wasn't a snake, it had no head or forked tongue or anything, but it had the same sort of writhing look to it. We talk about the darkness as if it were all just one thing, a single dimension. It isn't like that at all when you really study it. There's a spectrum, from the faintest ash-grey, to the uttermost, dankest blackness. Then there's the odd thing, that you can often make out the familiar shapes in your room, coated in darkness, somehow changed; but the very night air itself also has a form, or forms, that you don't see during the day. Or so it seems to me, anyway. Well, I was sure of this shape."

Maldon nodded his head, as if to emphasise his certainty. Then he resumed.

"I dare say you're wondering about overwork . . . "

"Or drink," said Breckland, succinctly.

"But in fact I was quite alert, and my tingling fear at the thing forming in the darkness was also accompanied by curiosity. I didn't in the least like what I was seeing, but I also wanted to know what it was. And that was what stopped my fingers from reaching out to put on the lamp, not that I think it would have made any difference. I suspect even in the half-light the swirl of darkness would still have been there. Because, apart from anything else, it was beginning to become a more definite form, it was shaping itself. It was becoming something I'd seen it in manuscripts: a sort of long 'z', or a '3', with a flourish of a tail . . . "

And he made a gesture, describing in the air what he meant. The fire leapt a little.

"And this thing lunged at me. It cavorted in front of my eyes, extending itself, then contracting, and the sort of pronged tail seemed to flicker angrily, as a cat's will. But as I watched, in a morbid fascination, I knew that the form in the darkness was familiar.

"And, strange as it may seem, I knew the name of my shadowy assailant."

"Its name?" I repeated.

"Yes. Yogh." He said the word with a distinct short hiss at the end.

"Sounds like some primeval demon," I suggested.

Maldon smiled. "Yes, doesn't it? But it wasn't that. Anyway, as soon as I knew what it was, I named it; I stared at it hard, and made the sighing sound myself, several times. Over and over in fact. I wasn't sure what would happen. For a while I was still faced with the shape in the darkness, slowly spiralling, as if poised. And then I began to sense a diminishing. There was a shift in the atmosphere—I no longer felt like, well, *prey*, and it seemed gradually to fade away. I did put the light on then, to make sure it was quite gone. And, yes, Breckland, I did then have a drink, I can tell you.

"In the morning, I checked with the bursar about the previous occupants of my rooms. I had a notion already, you see. Sure enough, the one a while before me—apart from quite a few temporary stayers—was Waley, the palaeographer. 'Waley of Paley', as the wags used to call him. Then I went and had a look in the library, which I knew had been the reluctant beneficiary of his papers. I hadn't been through them before, even though he worked in my field, because—to tell the truth—everyone said he was a bit cracked in the end, and his stuff not worth looking at. And sure enough, there it all was, his bequest, tied up with string, unsorted in a box. It included what *he* thought of as his last great master work, *The History of Yogh*, together with a draft monograph, probably never published, entitled *A Call for the Return of Yogh*."

Breckland treated us to one of his own sighs, definitely veering on the exasperated.

"And what is, or was, Yogh?"

"Oh, it's a lost English letter. That's why I said A, B, C isn't as simple as it sounds. Our alphabet, you know, wasn't settled until quite late on. For a long while we had extra letters, now gone. One was called Yogh, but it was pronounced like this: '*jzh*'." Maldon made a brief sighing, softly hissing sound from the top of his mouth.

"That's only an approximation. It's one of those letters that was very subtle, almost silent, a rune originally of course. It was taken over in the end by aspects of J, Y, and Z, or 'Gh' together. But it sort of survives in a few place-names, such as at the start of Jervaulx, the abbey, or the village of Bozeat in Northants."

"And that was what you were hearing . . . " said Breckland, trying to bring the story to a conclusion.

"Yes, just so."

Maldon made the "j" of "just" sound like the letter he'd pronounced.

"Funny. But . . . "

"I asked a few of the older men about Waley. They told me they'd heard something about his absolute fascination with this lost letter. He used to buttonhole them about it whenever he could. It seems he had an idea that English was really missing something, since that letter had gone; some touch of poetry, I suppose. He also had strong ideas about the origins and occurrences of the letter, which were a bit at variance with the usual authorities. One of those he had crossed said to me that he became fiercely possessive; it got to the stage where Waley almost identified himself with the letter. He was obsessed about the exact pronunciation, and could often be heard trying it out under his breath."

"So that sound survived him, then, in your—his old— rooms," I said.

"That's how it seemed. Well, I must admit, leafing through his papers, I did become interested. I devoted a bit of time to putting them in order. There was a lot there of some value. In the end, after a great deal of persuading, I got the college to publish most of his *History*, and even add parts of his pamphlet as an appendix. Then, the sighs seemed almost to cease. Not completely—I still heard them now and then. But nothing like as often. I had the sense that maybe now Waley was more at rest."

"The rain is beginning to leave off a bit," said Breckland, standing at the window and looking out thoughtfully at the dwindling greyness of the day.

You Walk the Pages

Have you ever used the services of youwalkthe-pages. com? They offer the perfect gift for the romantic, the book-lover, and all those friends and family who just love to dream. They will send you a book bound in blue, red, or green leatherette, with gilt-style embellishments. It will be a famous book, like for example *Wuthering Heights* or *Treasure Island*. Oh yes, you say, gift classics are nothing new, so what? Well, when your special person opens the book, what do they find? They find they are the hero or the heroine! That's right, instead of the actual name of the character they read their own name all the way through. You can imagine how different, how much more thrilling the book must seem when it is you who is having the adventures or the romance or whatever. At first it might seem funny but after a while people become really absorbed and they forget there was ever any other character and can only really imagine themselves in the book. Anyway, that is what they say. You can see what a great idea this is and how easy it is to do, really, for the geniuses behind youwalkthepages.com. Because all they have to do is to get an e-text of the classic book, and there are plenty of those around, and search-and-replace the original character with your choice of that special person. Then they just get it printed and nicely bound up.

But I soon had a different idea. You see there are people in this world who have not been very nice to me. I have got a list of them I have made. It has got a black border drawn around it in a big thick line; and in the box this makes, that is where I put their name. For example, there is my landlord Mr. Worrall. He was very rude to me when I was late with the rent a few times and also he is lazy about getting things repaired when they go wrong. There is damp in one corner of the room and it is spreading a grey patch on the wall and I have to look at it a lot as I am here in my room a lot and I do not want to look at it. So I asked him to come and get the leak fixed or whatever it is and he does not come to do that.

Then there is the girl in the chip shop with her pink greasy overall and her sweaty face. When I went there, which I do maybe once a week or so, I asked her if she would add to the bag some chippings. You know, they are the bits of fried batter that get left at the bottom of the pan and they are quite nice and crunchy and most places if you ask them will just scoop some up and put them in your bag for free without saying anything about it. But this girl said to me what do you mean chippings very loudly and made me look stupid in front of the other people in the queue and I did not know how to explain and so I did not get any, and now whenever I go in and she is there, I am sure she is giving me a stare. This is bad of her: she should know her trade and it must have been obvious what I mean—chippings—everyone knows those. But now I do not like to ask for any.

Also there is the old man, "the Doc" they call him, I do not know what he is a doctor of, but I do not think it is medicine, most probably not. He takes snuff which smells of moth-balls, and he sits at the table in the library and spreads out the newspapers all across it, he does not care if anyone else wants to sit there, and he spends most of the day there reading every single word, I am sure, of every single page, so there is never any room. I want to sit there and make notes, I only have a standard size spiral notebook, I do not need much space, but it is all I can do to get a little patch of the desk because of all the space he has got with his papers. He does not even look up, he does not give any sign that he sees you, or that you might want some space as well, you might as well not be there. If he saw what books I was looking at and what I was writing in my book, he might take a different attitude I believe.

Also there are strangers who look at me. I do not know who they are or what exactly they are thinking, but I can tell by the way they look at me that they are not having nice thoughts about me. Their eyes and their mouths and their noses are saying I do not like this person. What do they know when they only see my face and my hair and my clothes. All right I am not saying I am Heathcliff, exactly, I have got a face that is like a carved potato, lumpy, dingy, and I have got white hair that if I might continue the image you could say looks like an old potato when it sprouts, and as for what I wear I expect it hangs on me like potato sacks, so all around I am a walking vegetable, but they are not exactly the glittering mirrors of Versailles either, I can tell you, and so they do not have any call to look at me like that.

But as I was saying, what do they know when they only see my outside which I cannot help much. They should see my dreams. I have been making a list of everything that is known about the Seven Wonders of the World. One day I sat in my room wondering what to think about, what should engage a man who is a thinker and a dreamer, who is able to have visions like I am. And then it came to me all of a sudden that it was really very simple. If the ancients knew what were the greatest things in the world, which they did, why would I dwell upon anything else? The clue is all there for us. So first I made a list and soon found it is not as easy as you might think. I got the Pyramids and the Hanging Gardens of Babylon all right, and I remembered something about a colossus and a lighthouse, but then I started guessing and I soon saw I must be guessing wrong. But in the library, of course, they had a list and a bit of the history and the book also explained why there are seven, because the ancients always thought seven was a magical number. They are right about that, I think, because when I go off on my journeys with the numbers, I find seven walks fast and thinks high thoughts, whereas eight just sort of rolls along and is always looking for something to eat, and two is like a swan and just wants to glide on the water, very graceful but not actually doing anything.

The Seven Wonders were not always the same it seems, but in the end they got together a real list where everyone was agreed about what the seven were and that is the list I use. Then, when I had the list, I used a gold fibre pen to embellish it with symbols and I began working through each Wonder, one by one, finding out all I could about it, when it was built, what it looked like, what it was used for. There are websites as well as books about them, but in the end I found they often say the same things. My notebook did not get filled very fast. So then it dawned upon me that it might be my mission to be the man who really understands the meaning of the Seven Wonders and therefore I would stop writing notes about them and start thinking about them. So this is what I do. I stand at the foot of the Wonder and I look up and I see the light around it, which is a different coloured light for each one, I know they each have their own colour, and as I look at the coloured light it is as if I am inside the Wonder, I am exploring it, they all have corridors and chambers, even the statues, and I am the first person to go inside them and find out what is within. So I know what the Colossus knows and what the light of the Pharos shows, and these people who look at me, you see, they do not know what I know.

Which brings me back to where I started and how I made use of the idea of youwalkthepages.com. Anyone can do this, I said to myself, but they do not have to all be heroes. They could be villains; some people might like to be villains. You could be Blind Pew or the Artful Dodger or Dr. Fu Manchu. But also you could be victims. I do not think many people would like to be victims. I went and found Edgar Allan Poe's story "The Pit and the Pendulum". I changed the narrator to Mr. Worrall. Wherever it said "I", it was an easy matter to put "Mr. Worrall" instead: "Mr. Worrall was sick—sick unto death with that long agony; and when they at length unbound him, and Mr. Worrall was permitted to sit, Mr. Worrall felt that his senses were leaving him. The sentence—the dread sentence of death—was the last of distinct accentuation which reached Mr. Worrall's ears." That made me laugh. Mr. Worrall in fact has hairy ears. They'd have to shout loud to get the death sentence past that fungus. When I read the story through with Mr. Worral in it instead of Poe's own narrator, it was very satisfactory except for one thing, the ending where he gets rescued from the very edge of the pit by the revolutionaries who arrive just in time. So I naturally changed the ending so that he plunges into the pit. Then I had to imagine what was in the pit as Poe does not exactly say. In fact actually I could imagine a different thing every day. It wasn't so much "you walk the pages" for Mr. Worrall, it was more like "you crawl the pages".

This was good and so then I went and found another horror story and put the girl in the chip shop who made me feel small about the chippings in it, and what she went through in that story you do not want to know, but by the end of it she would be offering me the crunchiest nicest chippings for life I will tell you. And then I found one about somebody who slowly turns to dust and I put "the Doc" in that because of the specks of snuff that drift off him and also the pace with which he turns the pages of the newspapers he spreads out all across the tables, very slowly after long looking, and so him very slowly turning to dust seemed the right thing. I did not have to change the ending of that story because it ended all right, although not for "the Doc". Imagine falling into dust and still feeling everything.

There are some offices on the way to the library and they had a clear out and in a skip, among the swivel chair with its stuffing coming out through a slit and the dirty blinds bent and crumpled like bones and the long tube of light that had gone grey, I found some old ledgers, long and black and ruled inside; and after I had shook the grit and debris off them I saw they said in red lettering on the outside "Appointments". I liked the sound of that so I took them. Then one by one I put in this book the stories. Some of them that were short I printed out at the library and pasted in, but others I wrote in by hand and soon I had a book that was just as good as those that youwalkthepages.com do, but in a different sort of way. I left space after the end of "The Pit and the Pendulum" for Mr. Worrall to have lots to do in the pit, I used a red pen to write in the fate of the girl in the chip shop, and after the end of the dust story I wrote lots of dots so that "the Doc's" feeling dust would keep on falling. And I kept adding stories, of course, as I saw people in the street who looked at me wrongly, or as I found others who were not quite kind to me. There are more than enough horror stories to accommodate them all and more than enough appointment books from the stash I found in the skip to write them all in.

I soon found I had to put the Seven Wonders aside a time, while I looked for other horror stories that would be suitable, especially for the strangers I see every day that look at me badly. I had to memorise their faces, a distasteful task but it had to be done, and I had to give them a name that seemed to suit them, and that would help me remember them, and then I had to find the right story to put them in. It wasn't as easy as you might think. In quite a few stories the people escape or else what they have to endure does not last for very long, and that was not what I had in mind at all. I had to work through quite a lot of books and online texts at the library to get just the right fate for them. After a while I even found just the right one for Mr. Worrall in the pit, by combining it with another story. Down there, deep down there, he himself became a damp stain and nothing more, a dank and dribbling damp stain, but one that was still after a fashion Mr. Worrall. Let's see how he likes it, I thought. It's bad enough to have to look at one all the time but what about if you actually became one?

But I began to miss the Seven Wonders of the World. And also I thought that I was not doing what it was my job to do, which is to find out the secrets of the Wonders, why it was that they were made, why it was that they were chosen, and what they were really for. I wanted to visit them again, but at the same time I did not want to stop my important work with the appointment books. Then I realised I could do both. I took the appointment books in both my hands and started thinking again, until once more I stood before one of the Wonders, the Tomb of Mausolus, whose colour is indigo. All around it that colour shone until I became part of the colour too, and then I was inside it, stalking through its great rooms and long, long passages and still carrying the books with me. The shadows shrank from my indigo flame and all the stones wore faces.

And then it was obvious why I was doing this and I felt the books change in my hands as if they were black lava but my hands were unharmed and I knew I could mould the books however I wanted. And all the people I had captured in the book were like all the wrong people there have ever been since the world began, always the same, the spoilers, the spiteful, the spurners, and the purpose of the Wonders was to shun them and say there are greater things, there are high and grand and strange and strong things and they will always tower over you, as I who carry the books will tower over you, and I saw that each of the Wonders was really a temple and the god within might be Osiris or Apollo or Diana or Lucifer, but really it was always the same god, and his name was Baal. And the purpose of the temples was to consume all the wrong people of the world, all their pitiful spirits all their hard, spitting, unkind ways. And as I walked in the Tomb of Mausolus, all clothed in indigo, I thought I saw ranks and ranks of appointment books, with their black spines and bindings, and I knew that Seven walked by my side, with his proud head, and we came at last to a gap in the wall, a niche, and in that gaping slot I placed my appointment books.

Mr. Worrall, the damp stain, still spreads his infinitely painful way in a cold white crust across my wall, the girl in the chip shop finds that she and the pink smock streaked with fat are becoming indistinguishable, and "the Doc" as day after day he turns the pages and sniffs, is crumbling to dust before my eyes, but it is a dust that still feels things.

And now I know that all of them, all of them, all of you, can be caught in the appointment books and be changed into damp and fat and dust for ever and ever, while those who know the secrets of the Wonders will smile and still soar high and wander always in the colours and the light and make all things happen as they ought to happen. I think most people are already in an appointment book as they deserve, but I have set this all down because I am prepared to believe that there are others who are destined for the Wonders and who will see in me what they should see. Therefore do not say you do not understand or say bad things about me unless you definitely want to end up in the appointment books too, unless you want to become damp and fat and dust and nothing else; but rather if you are real and true, nod your head here at the end and let the high things fill your eyes and maybe I will see you in the Wonders.

Acknowledgements

My thanks to the following editors and publishers
for the first appearance of these stories, as follows:

"The Adventure of the Green Skull"
was first published in *Sherlock Holmes: The Game's Afoot*,
edited by David Stuart Davies. Wordsworth, 2008.

"Prince Zaleski's Secret" was first published in
The Rite of Trebizond. Ex Occidente Press, 2008.

"The 1909 Proserpine Prize" and "The Axholme Toll"
were first published in *The Nightfarers*.
Ex Occidente Press, 2009.

"The Late Post" was first published (as "The Lingering")
in *The Silent Companion* No. 6 (2011),
edited by António Monteiro.

"An Incomplete Apocalypse" was first published
in *Dark World*, edited by Timothy Parker Russell.
Tartarus Press, 2013.

"The Seer of Trieste"
was first published as a chapbook.
Swan River Press, 2008.

"The Fall of the King of Babylon"
was first published in *Terror Tales of East Anglia*,
edited by Paul Finch. Gray Friar Press, 2012.

"The Other Salt" was first published in
Secret Europe. Ex Occidente Press, 2012.

"The Tontine of Thirteen" and "The Antioch Imperial"
were first published in *The Peacock Escritoire*.
Ex Occidente Press, 2011.

"Morpheus House" was first published in *Strange Tales III*,
edited by Rosalie Parker. Tartarus Press, 2009.

"Without Instruments" was first published in
The First Book of Classical Horror,
edited by D.F. Lewis. Megazanthus Press, 2012.

"Fire Companions" was first published in
The Ghosts & Scholars Book of Shadows,
edited by Rosemary Pardoe. Sarob Press, 2012.
It is a sequel to "Two Doctors" by M.R. James.

"Yogh" was first published in
The Ghosts & Scholars M.R. James Newsletter 23,
edited by Rosemary Pardoe (2013).

"You Walk the Pages" was first published in
The Horror Anthology of Horror Anthologies,
edited by D.F. Lewis. Megazanthus Press, 2011.

"The Return of Kala Persad" is previously unpublished.
The title character was created by Headon Hill in
The Divinations of Kala Persad and Other Stories (1895).

About the Author

Mark Valentine's stories have been selected for *Best British Short Stories* edited by Nicholas Royle, *Best New Horror* edited by Stephen Jones, *The Mammoth Books of Ghost Stories* edited by Richard Dalby, and the *Ghosts & Scholars* books edited by Rosemary Pardoe, as well as for many other anthologies. Along with Swan River Press, he also publishes with other independent imprints such as Tartarus Press (UK), Sarob Press (France), and Zagava (Germany). His books include studies of Arthur Machen and the diplomat and fantasist Sarban, and essays on book-collecting and the esoteric. He also edits *Wormwood*, a journal of the fantastic.

SWAN RIVER PRESS

Founded in 2003, Swan River Press is an independent publishing company, based in Dublin, Ireland, dedicated to gothic, supernatural, and fantastic literature. We specialise in limited edition hardbacks, publishing fiction from around the world with an emphasis on Ireland's contributions to the genre.

www.swanriverpress.ie

"Handsome, beautifully made volumes . . . altogether irresistible."

– Michael Dirda, *Washington Post*

"It [is] often down to small, independent, specialist presses to keep the candle of horror fiction flickering . . . "

– Darryl Jones, *Irish Times*

"Swan River Press has emerged as one of the most inspiring new presses over the past decade. Not only are the books beautifully presented and professionally produced, but they aspire consistently to high literary quality and originality, ranging from current writers of supernatural/weird fiction to rare or forgotten works by departed authors."

– Peter Bell, *Ghosts & Scholars*

SELECTED STORIES

Mark Valentine

"Nothing lasts! The faun sleeps,
Smiling, mute, remorseless."

– Ludmila Jevsejeva, *Autuna Melodio*

In St. Petersburg, amidst an uneasy truce with the revolution, there exists a secret trade in looted ikons. But who are the dark strangers seeking for the Gate of the Archangel? In the small town of Tzern, news arrives of the death of the Emperor; meanwhile a postmaster, a priest, a prophet and a war-wearied soldier watch the dawn for signs of the future. Constantinople: A quest for the lost faiths of the former Ottoman Empire leads a French scholar to believe that the strangest may also be the truest. On the edges of Europe, exiles and idealists meet in a café to talk of their hopes—while sinister forces begin to march. These stories, exquisitely told by Mark Valentine, are about individuals caught up in the endings of old empires—and of what comes next.

"Valentine is a master at capturing the ineffable in prose,
of writing stories that combine a gentle plot, an unusual
setting and a character filled with longing to create an effect
that describes aspects of the world, aspects of our lives that
simply cannot be addressed in any straightforward fashion."

– *The Agony Column*

THE SILVER VOICES

John Howard

Transylvania: the country beyond the forest and land of the seven fortress towns. In *The Silver Voices* we encounter the previously unknown eighth town: Sternbergstadt. Now known as Steaua de Munte, it's one of those places where past and present continually meet, with no-one being entirely sure which has the upper hand. In Steaua de Munte history can never be said to be dead and buried; it plays too many tricks on the present and future for that.

"*Sad . . . with an elegiac quality commemorating all that was lost to the war, the ways in which the world changed for better and worse.*"

– *Black Static*

"*Ambiguity does not stop with the work's overall composition but proceeds to infect each of the stories . . . Such is the hallmark of gifted writing.*"

– *Dead Reckonings*

THE SEA CHANGE
& Other Stories

Helen Grant

In her first collection, award-winning author Helen Grant plumbs the depths of the uncanny: Ten fathoms down, where the light filtering through the salt water turns everything grey-green, something awaits unwary divers. A self-aggrandising art critic travelling in rural Slovakia finds love with a beauty half his age—and pays the price. In a small German town, a nocturnal visitor preys upon children; there is a way to keep it off—but the ritual must be perfect. A rock climber dares to scale a local crag with a diabolical reputation, and makes a shocking discovery at the top. In each of these seven tales, unpleasantries and grotesqueries abound—and Grant reminds us with each one that there can be fates even worse than death.

"A brilliant chronicler of the uncanny as only those who dwell in places of dripping, graylit beauty can be."

– Joyce Carol Oates

"Meticulously written and with carefully calculated chills."

– *Black Static*